Snake's Pillow and Other Stories

Fiction from Modern China

This series is intended to showcase new and exciting works by China's finest contemporary novelists in fresh, authoritative translations. It represents innovative recent fiction by some of the boldest new voices in China today as well as classic works of this century by internationally acclaimed novelists. Bringing together writers from several geographical areas and from a range of cultural and political milieus, the series opens new doors to twentieth-century China.

Howard Goldblatt

General Editor

General Editor, Howard Goldblatt

Zhu Lin

Snake's Pillow

and Other Stories

Translated from the Chinese by Richard King

University of Hawai'i Press
Honolulu

Printed in the United States of America
03 02 01 00 99 98 5 4 3 2 1

Library of Congress Cataloging-in-Publication Data

Chu, Lin, 1949–
[Short stories. English. Selections]
Snake's pillow and other stories / Zhu Lin ; translated from the Chinese by Richard King.
p. cm. — (Fiction from modern China)
ISBN 0-8248-1549-1 (alk. paper). —
ISBN 0-8248-1716-8 (pbk. : alk. paper)
1. Chu, Lin, 1949– —Translations into English.
I. King, Richard. II. Title. III. Series.
PL2852.L54A24 1998
895.1'352—dc21 97-37519
CIP

University of Hawai'i Press books are printed on acid-free paper and meet the guidelines for permanence and durability of the Council on Library Resources

Designed by Barbara Pope Book Design
based on the series design by Richard Hendel

Contents

Snake's Pillow

—1—

From a distance, the river was hardly visible. A faint haze hung over the water, and bamboo groves on the bank, emerald green in spring, cast their reflections on its surface. The water by the dock where she sat was so luminous and soft, so clear and sparkling, that it seemed like . . . like her own pure and gentle heart, the heart of the girl called Rice-Basket.

Hers was not a pretty name, not really a name at all. Can a person be called "Rice-Basket"? Yet the hopes and blessings of two generations were invested in this name. Mother wanted her to be blessed all her life, prosperous as a rice basket filled to overflowing; Grandma wanted her to be generous as the rice basket, which provides constant nourishment to mankind.

On long winter nights, Grandma sat at home spinning thread. As she spun she would tell little Rice-Basket tales of fairies and demons, of nymphs and dryads, of karma and retribution. The pure white strands she spun never broke, and she never ran out of stories.

All Grandma's stories seemed to conclude with the words, "Amithaba Buddha, to be human you must show goodness."

Once Rice-Basket, curious, looked up at her with jet-black eyes: "Must you show goodness to wicked people as well?"

"You must still show goodness."

"Why?"

"Goodness will be rewarded with goodness."

After a moment's thought, Grandma added, "And if you don't find your reward in this life, you surely will in the next."

Little Rice-Basket cupped her cheeks in her hands, her fine black eyes as docile and appealing as a lamb's: "Your stories are so good, Grandma, tell me another one. . . ."

Day and night, Slanting Brook flowed past their door, its gentle plashing echoing into the vastness above, redolent with dreams of lives to come.

Rice-Basket grew up and blossomed, like jasmine sweetly fragrant in the glistening dew. She no longer believed in lives to come or in retribution, but she still stayed true to the code that Grandma had taught her. She venerated her elders and cared for children, and the tranquil beauty of her smile, like the first soft rays of morning sun after rain, brought joy to all who saw it.

In spring the waters of Slanting Brook swelled like a girl blossoming into womanhood, clapping and stamping, springing and leaping, merrily brushing the grassy banks with her dress. Spray from the brook formed a dense mist in the bamboo grove and wove a green carpet there as luxuriant as Rice-Basket's raven hair.

Rains came, drifting in fine strands on the wind, floating through the bamboo grove and into the branches of the silk and elm trees. After the rain had passed, a moist pungency permeated the air. Wildflowers of all colors burst from the banks like mischievous girls, decked in red, yellow, purple, or white; they peeped shyly from the green waves of the meadow, revealing their bright colors to the sun.

Her feet bare but for straw sandals, Rice-Basket cut grass

along the riverbank. Behind the bamboo grove there was a patch of shade, where ancient willows and chinaberries hung over the narrow river, making the grass damp and chilly, so that if it hadn't been for that one kind of flower thrusting forth from the lush green carpet . . . and what a delicate, entrancing flower! Devoid of thorns or petals, it offered up its flaming heart, thrusting forth on a slender stem the most precious part of its existence—a cluster of nectar-filled orbs the color of fresh blood. When it blossomed in the spring rains, it scattered a profusion of rubies over the shady, secluded pastures.

Rice-Basket loved the flower's red freshness, loved the flower's round fullness, loved it for blooming where others would not grow. She often felt that were it not for that flower, the venerable trees, the forgotten bamboo, and the wild grasses would feel lonely and isolated. Yet this flower had a most unpleasant name—it was called the snake's pillow flower.

Sometimes when Rice-Basket tired of cutting grass, she would pluck a snake's pillow, playfully tucking it between her fingers like an engagement ring. Her friends would be shocked when they saw it: "You mustn't pick the snake's pillow, or a snake will bite you! Don't you know the legend?"

Rice-Basket would smile and nod, but she still picked a few of the flowers from time to time, placing them in a chipped mug that she kept by the north window of her room.

Opposite Rice-Basket's window stood a ramshackle gray hut, and in the hut lived Blind Aqian and his big fool of a son. Aqian wasn't completely blind—one eye could see a little—but he'd never been keen on working. On bright and breezy autumn days, the good-natured team leader would call him out to sit in the warm sun and sieve the husks from the grain to earn a few work points, but Aqian paid no attention. When buds were swelling in the spring warmth, people would come to drag him off to stretch his limbs and get some exercise hoeing the earth around the rape plants with the married women, but he would glower at them with his one good eye. Then he would eat his fill, slump down on his rickety bed, and sleep, drooling long gobs of spittle.

Aqian made his living from a patch of bamboo behind his home, which he had inherited from his father. It needed no plowing or sowing. Bountiful nature watered it with spring rain and autumn dew, sent sunlight and breezes, so that year by year the plants grew taller and put out new shoots. Every three years he would harvest the bamboo, making more than a thousand yuan from the sale.

With this kind of income, it shouldn't have been too difficult for Aqian to get himself a clever and capable wife, if only he'd been more of a worker and kept himself a bit cleaner. But that just wasn't his way. He only ever ate from one bowl, and he never washed it. When he finished a meal, he just dropped the bowl on the counter with his chopsticks underneath it. In summer and autumn, bugs would crawl in between the chopsticks to form a black layer at the bottom of the bowl. During the campaign to wipe out the four pests, schoolchildren fought with each other for the right to catch bugs in his bowl so that they could add to the tally they reported at school. He was lucky the bowl didn't get smashed.

Aqian loved to eat meat. Not that anyone had ever seen him buy fresh tender pork ribs or a solid piece of ham. He even spurned cheaper cuts like pig's feet and offal. Every couple of weeks he would walk the few miles to the market town (the bus ride would have cost him twenty cents) and come back with a dripping-red pig's head, which he would chop up and fry. He would leave the meat lying out for several days at a time, even in summer, but it never made him sick.

When he had to do something, he would reinforce the fence around his bamboo grove. The fence was solid and closely woven so that children and animals were kept well clear—not even an ant would have been able to sneak in to nibble a blade of grass. Yet somehow a clump of the good-hearted snake's pillow managed to bloom blood-red inside this cold and forbidding compound.

No one would ever have guessed that this fresh and vibrant redness would have such an effect on Aqian's shadowy vision, but all of a sudden he began to harbor thoughts of love and to yearn for a wife. Since he wasn't prepared to part with a cent for bride-price, and nobody local would have him, he ended up taking in a half-witted woman who had fled famine in the north to beg for food.

The half-witted woman brought along her dimwit son. For the wedding, all Aqian did was to feed mother and son a bowl of pig's head; otherwise not a penny was spent. But afterward Aqian discovered he had made a bad bargain—the half-witted woman couldn't do anything useful but still expected to eat, so now he had two more mouths to feed. The more he thought about it, the angrier he felt. Often he refused to feed them, turning them out by day to beg and only letting them back in at night to sleep.

In due course the half-witted woman died, and her dimwit son grew into a strapping young fellow. He didn't have a name, so the neighbors called him Big Fool, or else Dead-Loss Fool. Big Fool rambled around the village all day, unkempt and disheveled, bare skin showing through his tattered clothing. He would pilfer a melon from one family, a stalk of corn from another, to sustain his robust health.

Big Fool was the only one in this simple village who was permitted to get away with theft. Even the stingiest of people didn't stand in his way when he came to steal; sharp-tongued women, who would normally raise an almighty row if a wilted rice stalk went missing, would just sigh when told that it was Dead-Loss Fool who did it: "Ah well, what can you do? We mustn't let him starve."

Sometimes the people he had stolen from would call him over with a laugh, "Big Fool, if you're going to pinch stuff from my place, you can fetch me some water to make amends." Or else, "Go on, cut me a basket of grass as your penance."

Big Fool was always happy to perform such tasks. He would just chuckle at their talk, and if they gave him a bowl of rice topped with pickled vegetables, he would have their water vat filled to the brim in no time, or he'd pack grass into their basket so tightly that it seemed to have grown right in there.

Rice-Basket felt sorry for Big Fool. She saw that he went barefoot in all seasons, so she made him shoes. When his clothes were worn, she stitched and patched them. Because of this, Big Fool treated her with great respect. He might steal from everyone else, but he'd never take so much as a sprig of chives from her.

One day Big Fool went wandering off, rambling farther afield than usual, until he ended up in a melon patch. The muskmelons were ripening, their heady fragrance filling the air, and Big Fool's mouth watered. He sneaked off with an armful and sat down beside the road, slurping noisily.

The people here didn't know about Big Fool; besides, they had lost a number of melons recently. The old man who guarded the melons flew into a rage when he saw what was happening and summoned some younger fellows, who rushed over and jumped on Big Fool.

When Big Fool saw people coming to grab him, he hadn't the wit to run away, but simply closed his eyes tight and let them tie him up. Since he offered no resistance, Big Fool was soon securely bound to a stone pillar. The furious watchman picked up a carrying pole, determined to work off his fury by giving Big Fool a sound thrashing. Big Fool had probably never suffered such pain, but he didn't know how to plead for mercy. His stolid face expressionless, his foolish eyes perplexed, he gazed in dismay at the crowd of onlookers.

It so happened that Rice-Basket was in that village to visit her maternal grandmother. When she saw what was happening, she dashed over to explain that this was just a poor simpleton, pulling out money to compensate them for the melons. They untied Big Fool.

"Come on," said Rice-Basket. "Let's go home."

And, miraculously, that great brawny ox Big Fool followed Rice-Basket without a word, docile as a little child.

"Big Fool, you've been thieving again!" Rice-Basket scolded him, in the usual village way.

Big Fool didn't respond with his habitual foolish snigger. He just hung his head and walked dumbly on.

Rice-Basket smiled. "Big Fool, is it right to steal?"

Big Fool looked up. His dull eyes widened, staring quizzically at Rice-Basket.

"Tell me, is it right?" She frowned with unwitting charm.

Big Fool's head quivered slightly, but it was hard to tell whether he was nodding or shaking it.

Rice-Basket chuckled, "It's not right for you to steal. It's shameful to take people's things. Promise me you won't steal anymore."

Big Fool clearly and distinctly nodded his head.

"A big strong fellow like you ought to be working for the collective, earning his living through labor. That's the honorable way," Rice-Basket said.

"Labor . . . honorable. . . ." Stumblingly he repeated her words.

"Hooray!" Rice-Basket clapped her hands with glee. "I'll talk to the team leader, and he can let you look after a buffalo. Then you'll earn work points, and in the autumn you'll be given grain like everyone else, all right?"

Big Fool nodded vigorously, though heaven only knows whether he'd really understood what Rice-Basket had said.

Back in the village, Big Fool did indeed take a buffalo out

to pasture. A delighted team leader told everyone he saw, "It's all thanks to Rice-Basket's goodness that we're making an honest man of Big Fool."

—3—

Would Rice-Basket's goodness be rewarded with goodness as Grandma had promised? The answer to this question remained a mystery.

However, there was one result that everyone could see. Having become renowned for her goodness, Rice-Basket found her doorstep worn down by the feet of matchmakers carrying proposals of marriage. In this new age when young wives bullied their mothers-in-law, who wouldn't want a daughter-in-law who was docile and kindly and respected her elders?

But as these joyful expectations arose, malevolent desire was also stirring. It made Rice-Basket feel insecure. At work or at rest, taking a stroll or attending a meeting, she was often aware of a pair of burning eyes trained greedily on her. It wasn't in her nature to confront someone with an angry look; all she could do was scurry away like a frightened rabbit.

Rice-Basket was not the only one to fear this glare; it frightened her parents and the other villagers as well. This man was at the center of authority in the brigade, and in these disordered times he held the power of life and death in his hands. When he too came to propose marriage, Rice-Basket's parents summoned all their courage and tremblingly turned him down. Their reasons were simple enough—they didn't think he would treat their daughter well, and they also knew that, although he was still quite young, he was a frequent visitor to houses of ill repute. Rice-Basket thanked her parents for protecting her, and from that time on she never went out on her own by day, staying at home with the door barred.

Her heart, of course, could not be barred. In the darkness of her little room, she too dreamed sweet romantic dreams.

Mystical and enchanted as these dreams were, they were at the same time quite practical. Her quiet longing was that some day her father and mother would select some honest and well-favored lad. Then her mother would close the door and ask her with a wry smile, "Well?" And she would hang her head and shyly whisper, "Whatever you think best, Mama." Satisfied, her mother would nod her head and leave. And in the months and years that followed, the sweat of honest toil would water land that was shared in love. . . .

When she opened the window early in the morning, the verdant bamboo grove was sheathed in drifting mist, turning it into a mysterious land of illusion. Then the birdsongs started, first one, "chirrup, chirrup," light and timid to sound things out, then followed soon after by a joyful chorus of birds who understood that morning had broken and it was time for them to congregate. The light of dawn unfurled in waves, bathing the bamboo groves in a warm rose pink.

Rice-Basket sat in silence, her whole heart suffused with a feeling of belonging, a feeling like a fresh caress. Then she glanced down and caught sight of a freshly plucked snake's pillow in the chipped mug. The flower was tender and bright, early sunlight glinting on the dewdrops that still clung to its petals, like a glistening chip of red coral. Where had it come from? Curious, she bent and brushed it with her lips. So delicate was the scent that it seemed the scarlet orb was not so much fragrant as radiant with the essence of new life. Enchanted, Rice-Basket pressed her face into the flower's roundness.

Who had picked the flower? Who had put it in her mug? Was he handsome and appealing? As she pondered, the faces of several young men she knew flickered before her eyes. At first it was gay and fun, but then she felt alarmed and ashamed of her reckless imaginings, her cheeks blushing to the same glorious hue as the round flower.

In a while, she thought, she should fetch a basket of grass

for her lambs and rabbits and then do the family laundry before she went off to work. She tossed her head back and ran a wooden comb through her thick hair. Then she noticed someone standing in front of the bamboo grove.

She started, realizing that he might have seen into her most intimate feelings. Flustered, she dropped the comb. When she picked it up and looked again, he was still standing there motionless, more like a statue than a man. When she gathered herself and looked more closely, she saw that it was Big Fool! Big Fool's trouser legs were soaked through, and his tousled hair was dripping. He might have been standing there for ages.

Rice-Basket's racing heart relaxed. She gave Big Fool a gentle caring gaze. Big Fool stared unblinking at her.

"Big Fool, what are you doing here?" she asked. Her manner was surprised but still friendly.

Big Fool said nothing, but he kept on staring at her intently. "Moo. . . ." The sound came from Big Fool's water buffalo.

Rice-Basket shook her comb at him: "Be off with you, Big Fool. Take your buffalo out to pasture!"

Big Fool simpered; then he slapped the buffalo on the rump. "Haw!" he shouted, and led the buffalo away, his burly frame disappearing awkwardly around the emerald bamboo grove.

"Labor . . . honorable! Labor . . . honorable!" The muffled voice filtered through the rustling green leaves in tune with the antiphony of birdsong.

The corners of Rice-Basket's mouth turned up in a kindly smile.

—4—

There is seldom time to be lonely in the fields of Jiangnan. Working is a cheerful business.

Big Fool took to his new job with the same diligence he had always shown when cutting grass or fetching water. The team leader said, "Big Fool, don't steal or idle. Don't leave your buffalo in one place too long, or the grass will get spoiled." So Big Fool and his buffalo ranged far and wide, going wherever the grass was tender, and by evening the old buffalo's stomach was bulging.

The team leader said, "Big Fool, whatever you do, don't let the buffalo eat snails, or he'll get the bloated-belly disease and die." So Big Fool carefully inspected all the grass he cut for the buffalo, picking out snails and even ants and throwing them aside.

From time to time when he was hungry, he'd still go to the fields or to someone's garden to pick a handful of fruit or cut a stick of sugarcane. When the owners saw this, they would say, as usual, "Big Fool, you've been thieving again!" Then Big Fool would hang his head and drop his arms, needlessly stroking the buffalo's back. The owners would laugh, "Ho, I won't punish you—after all, you're a workingman now!"

In no time it was June. Dust billowed on the highway, and the sultry midday heat dragged on interminably. Big Fool did as the team leader instructed, leading the old water buffalo to wash in the brook down by the willows. At the first touch of the clear cool water, the buffalo would roll over in delight, and Big Fool would also tumble splashing into the water, washing himself as well as the buffalo. After a bath, the old buffalo was always full of energy. Big Fool also seemed livelier when he was clean; he would put on the clothes that Rice-Basket had patched for him and look quite normal. People who were idling away their siesta among the willows joked back and forth:

"Big Fool, you look so cute, are you getting married today?"

"Big Fool, do you want me to fix you up with a wife?"

"Big Fool, life's just great when you've got a wife. There's someone to mend your clothes in the day and someone to go to bed with at night."

Puzzled, Big Fool looked from one to the other, as though

trying to work out the meaning of the word *wife* in their mockery.

"Sure, there's a girl in West Village who's a half-wit. Do you want her, Big Fool?" someone asked jovially.

Soundlessly Big Fool ran his fingers through the buffalo's dripping coat.

"Hoho, he's setting his sights higher than that. He wouldn't want her," someone called with mock disdain.

"Who do you fancy, Big Fool?"

"Could it be Rice-Basket?"

Another chorus of laughs. Big Fool abruptly looked up. His bleary eyes shone with joy, like a parched field when a breeze blows across it.

"Rice-Basket, Rice-Basket. . . ," he murmured.

The laughter became even more malicious: "Does Rice-Basket look after you all right?"

"Does Rice-Basket fancy you?"

Big Fool rolled his eyes. After a while he scratched his head and said, "Rice-Basket treasures me."

The laughter subsided, and a voice said with newfound respect, "Hey! Big Fool's no fool!"

This was true enough—the reply had been precise, intelligent, and to the point.

The word *treasure* in the local dialect does not mean love; it conveys sympathy, pity, and concern.

—5—

In the deepening haze of dusk, the village became a land of illusion. The gold of the ripened wheat, the deep turquoise of the beans, the lush greenery of willows and bamboos, and the pink of the catkins on the silk tree, all dissolved in the blur of the evening mists. Even the grimy walls of Aqian's shabby hut blurred and could no longer be distinguished from Rice-Basket's bright and cheerful room.

When Big Fool was finished with the buffalo, he stood dumbly in the shadow of the bamboos, looking across at Rice-Basket's window. She was still at work in the fields; gaily colored clothes had been hung out to dry on a bamboo pole sticking out of the window and fluttered desultorily in the breeze.

Someone, dark as the shadows, was lurking beneath Rice-Basket's window.

"Who's there? You, standing there, who are you?" It was the other man, not Big Fool, that started with fright. Anyone else who saw him would have addressed him respectfully, but Big Fool didn't feel obliged.

"Dead-Loss Fool!" cursed the man when he saw who was there. He spat out the stub of his cigarette and stalked off. Suddenly he changed his mind. Leaning against a sequoia tree he lit another cigarette. "Big Fool, come here a minute," he beckoned.

Big Fool ignored him. But the man took no offense, strolling over and patting Big Fool on the shoulder.

"Is Rice-Basket nice? Does she like you?"

"Hee-hee," came Big Fool's giggled response.

"Go on then, pick something off her pole and take it home," he said.

Big Fool shook his head unwillingly.

"Go on," laughed the man, pushing Big Fool forward. "If you take Rice-Basket's clothes, she'll be your wife—and you do want a wife, don't you?"

Big Fool stood dull, immobile. Suddenly a sharp gust of wind blew a pair of red and white patterned undershorts down from the pole. The man walked over, bent down, and picked them up; he stroked them a few times before pressing them into Big Fool's massive hand: "Here, Rice-Basket has given them to you to wear."

Big Fool licked his lips with delight as he took them. He believed what the man said because Rice-Basket really did give him things sometimes, like shoes and clothes.

The man walked off and disappeared into the darkness. The setting sun glowed brighter in a sapphire sky, salmon strands of cloud shimmering overhead. Big Fool clasped to his breast the softness that the man had given him, whispering, "Treasure . . . treasures me . . . Rice-Basket. . . ."

—6—

Big Fool was beaming the next day as he set out with the buffalo for the pasture, wearing the red and white undershorts.

There was bedlam in the village. Everyone came rushing out to witness this extraordinary event, young and old, men and women, youngsters toting hoes, women carrying babies, schoolchildren with satchels, and bare-bottomed toddlers. They couldn't have been more excited if the news had been that grain was falling from the sky or that gold bars were growing on the trees.

Unaware of the chaos he was causing, Big Fool stood straight and tall outside Rice-Basket's window, still wearing the red and white undershorts. Rice-Basket's father, a man so gentle he wouldn't crush an ant, went crazy with anger. Gnashing his teeth, he charged up to Big Fool and laid into him with a carrying pole. Thwack! Thwack! The blows lashed crisply into flesh, but Big Fool stood still, unflinching and uncomplaining, bewilderment in his eyes.

The old man's fury was unabated; but his hands weakened, and the pole dropped to the ground. Only then did Big Fool shamble off, his head in his hands. As he reached the bamboo grove, he crashed to the ground like a felled tree, his bleeding body sullying the fresh full blooms of the snake's pillow flowers.

—7—

Summer passed into autumn. The guest chair in Rice-Basket's house was gray with dust, as matchmakers no longer came to pay their respects. Her poor father and mother looked at each other and sighed in despair.

By day, Rice-Basket went out to work in the fields, where an expanse of withered leaves shrouded the pure white cotton bolls. As the solitary girl picked cotton, cold gusts of malice from behind her back wafted into her ears on the unfeeling wind.

"Hee-hee, what a fresh little blossom to bed down with a Big Fool. . . ."

"What do you mean blossom; more likely she's a fox-fairy in human form."

"You'd never have known it; she always seemed such a good sort."

"Huh, that was just an act to fool us all!"

The cotton bolls spun and shook before her, light and pale, slight and gleaming, like clouds, like mist, collecting and dispersing like the first flickering rays of dawn. Only by pinching herself sharply between thumb and forefinger did she prevent herself from fainting.

In the evening, when she went down to the river with her basket to wash rice and rinse vegetables, her former friends would scatter, sniggering behind their hands. Head bowed, she dropped tears of shame and anger into the river's icy fastness.

In the still of the night she sat by her loom, weaving into cloth the thread that her dead grandmother had spun. The monotonous "clack, clack" of the old loom, like an ancient unending dirge, struck a chord in her lonely grieving heart.

As the gossip spread, pain and resentment clogged the joy of youth and the sweet dreams of girlhood. Slanting Brook gurgled on day and night outside her door, ridiculing the admonitions to goodness in the tales that Grandma had told little Rice-Basket so many years before. But good and evil in the world of men cannot change the logic of beauty, and Rice-Basket was as lovely as ever. When she filled her buckets as the first rays of morning sun fell on the surface of the river, the water reflected her elegant figure. But at times it would also reflect a pair of lustful eyes concealed among the willows.

One night the barred door of Rice-Basket's room was torn open. Not by her parents—they had been sent by the brigade authorities to dig earth at an irrigation project a good way away, far enough that they had to stay there overnight. It was him—his eyes gleaming in the darkness, like a predator about to seize a lamb, his harsh panting like a savage summer storm. Once in the room, he turned and barred the door behind him.

Rice-Basket made a dash for the door. Self-preservation gave her sudden strength, letting her wrench the bar from the door, but still it wouldn't open—it had been bolted from the outside as well. In her despair, Rice-Basket screamed for help. Her cries were slight and feeble in the darkness of the night. None dared to offend the holder of supreme power or heed the cries of a fallen woman. Her neighbor Blind Aqian fumbled to light a fire to stew the pound of pigs' tails that was his reward for bolting her door.

The pitiful Rice-Basket trembled, like a bamboo leaf in the west wind, like the little flower that pillows the viper's head. In that instant she thought of Big Fool. If only he were there, he might have saved her. But Big Fool had been locked in his room by his blind father, another favor paid for with the pigs' tails.

"Aargh. . . ."

Suddenly, somewhere, a roar sounded, a muffled furious roar like that of a cornered beast. Unlike Rice-Basket's plaintive call for help, this was a roar of irresistible brute force. Rice-Basket's spirits revived; the man took fright for a second. But then he realized that this noise was no threat to him and leaped forward once again. . . .

Then came a hammering at the door. The man looked round as the flimsy door began to shake in a shower of dust, rocked by a pair of mighty hands.

"Aargh!" The furious roar was heard again, this time from the other side of the door. The force of the sound almost bowled them over. Then the door crashed to the ground, and a figure appeared in the doorway. It was Big Fool! One foot was on the fallen door. His eyes were bloodshot, his hair standing on end. Even in late autumn, he wore only a pair of shorts; shadowy moonlight played on his brawny naked form, savagely beautiful like that of some prehistoric man.

The man backed off, awed by such strength. Big Fool strode forward and seized him, then hoisted him easily over his shoulder like a sack of flour and carried him out. There was a splash from the riverbank as Big Fool hurled him in. It was just as well the man was a strong swimmer, or he might have drowned. Still, he had swallowed several mouthfuls of water before he managed to crawl out.

Rice-Basket's reputation got even worse after this incident. It all stood to reason: Why had the man picked on Rice-Basket and not one of the other girls? Everyone knows that flies only buzz round cracked eggs, and whose fault was it but her own if she was defiled? And there was Big Fool acting the jealous lover too; that was another thing that everyone found titillating.

All Rice-Basket's father could do was look for anyone who would be prepared to arrange a marriage for their daughter.

Her new home was to be far away, in a place none of them had ever been. All they had heard was that high mountains squeezed the land into strips and cut the sky into pieces, constricting the spirits of those who dwelt there. It was also said that the people there were so poor that many could not afford the price of a bride, and women were scarce.

In the last rains of autumn, the blush faded from the face of the snake's pillow; its blooms withered, and its seeds buried themselves in the soil. Then it was that Rice-Basket went away in marriage.

The day of her departure was quite a festive one. The golden fruits of the chinaberry gleamed in the pale sunlight. Rice-Basket's parents prepared a modest feast, and their relatives came along to help out and eat. From early morning, Big Fool stood listlessly outside Rice-Basket's window. No matter how people pushed, they couldn't shift him; if they pushed too hard, he would roar in fury like a lion. No one could do anything with him, so they just left him alone.

Finally, firecrackers were set off, and as the smell of gunpowder hung in the air, Rice-Basket, wearing a new red dress, was lifted onto the back of a bicycle. Mother and father both began to weep. Rice-Basket swallowed back her tears, bowed her head, and looked away. The bicycle wheels began to spin round, firecrackers exploded festively, and the flutes, pipes, and woodwinds blared out their rowdy tunes of celebration.

Seemingly struck by some profound thought, Big Fool rushed a few paces forward. Someone offered him a bowl of rice piled with a glistening serving of red-fried pork and half a fish. He pushed it away without a second glance.

As the bicycle pulled farther away, the pinpoint of red faded into invisibility in the barren vastness of the open fields of early winter.

Big Fool slumped down, howling and sobbing into his hands, his crying like the baying of a wounded wolf. People glanced at each other. None of them had ever seen him cry before. Even when he'd been flogged half to death, he hadn't shed a tear, so what could be bothering him now?

Some well-meaning person asked him, "Big Fool, why are you crying?"

"There's nobody to treasure me anymore," he said, as two muddy streams of tears coursed down his grimy face.

—8—

Time slipped by, and the seasons gave way one to another. Rice-Basket's father and mother passed away; weeds covered Big Fool's grave. Strangely, Blind Aqian survived, though his bamboo grove was a wilderness, and his shack had collapsed. He could hardly move anymore, let alone walk the few miles to market to buy pig's head. He was now dependant on public charity for his welfare and hadn't eaten meat in ages.

One midday, a stranger came along the road to the village.

It was a woman, who looked to be in her forties, her hands and face weathered and coarse, with wrinkles on her forehead and around her eyes. She was dressed in clothes of blue cotton that were clean but out of style. With her came two children, the elder a girl of eight or nine, with a pretty round face; the younger, a boy, only five or six, had a mischievous tigerish look to him. Both wore new clothes—the girl's jacket was of patterned red corduroy, the boy's of blue twill. The children were alert and inquisitive, perhaps because the place was new to them. They tugged constantly at their mother's hand or ran whooping on ahead.

Just before they reached the village, the mother changed direction, following the stream toward a spot behind the bamboo grove. Exhaustedly she slumped down between two hillocks. Perhaps she realized that these were grave mounds, perhaps not. It was shaded there; the wind was cold and the water chilly. Ancient chinaberries stretched their gnarled limbs over the water. Wild grass grew thickly at their feet.

"Mama, look at the pretty flowers!" called the little girl, holding a cluster of glistening snake's pillow and threading the flowers one by one into her hair.

When the woman saw this, her expression changed. She snatched the flowers from her daughter's hair and hurled them to the ground as if they were evil.

The little girl wailed, "But they're so pretty, and we don't have them where we live. . . ."

"Be a good girl. Don't ask for the flowers, and I'll give you some candy," the woman said soothingly, drawing two pieces of sesame brittle from her pocket.

"I don't want candy, want flowers, want flowers. . . ," the headstrong girl persisted tearfully.

The little boy joined in, "Want flowers, want flowers."

"Darlings, this is called the snake's pillow flower. If you pick it, the snake will bite you." The woman bowed her head and pulled one of the tiny globes apart. Red nectar ran like blood through her fingers.

"Why, Mama?" The girl had stopped fussing and looked wide-eyed and curious at her mother.

"There's a story. . . ," said the mother, as the past flashed before her.

The wind blew up, scattering the seed heads of the dandelions, waving the hare grass back and forth, revealing glimpses of shining white ears of seed. Bamboos rustled in the grove beyond the graves. The mother's story began:

"Once upon a time, there was a snake, an idle good-for-nothing fellow, and an ugly one; nobody wanted to be friends with it, so it just roamed to and fro all day, alone in the bamboo grove.

"The bamboo grove was as lovely then as it is today, full of all sorts of flowers: lilies, chrysanthemums, thorned dog-roses, and thornless morning glories. The different flowers were young girls, some lively, some passionate, some playful, some gentle . . . but no matter which flower, no matter what the temperament of the girl, none would be married to the snake. So the snake was sad and alone in the world, with no friend or lover. It was worst of all in winter, when it just lay motionless and alone, nobody caring as its body froze.

"Of all the flowers, the freshest and fairest was a little red one, sweet and kind. Its blooms were round as rubies, its body moist and limpid, with no hurtful thorns. The little red flower felt pity for the snake's lot and became its wife.

"For the first few days the snake was delighted to have the little red flower. But before too long, its cruel nature began to show. It didn't care for its wife at all, treating her brutally, whipping her and crushing her under its head as a pillow—that's the origin of the name *snake's pillow* that people later gave to the little red flower.

"One day the wicked snake was caught by a hunter. He took a sharp knife to cut the snake open and take out its gallbladder—it's a medicine, the best cure for convulsions.

"When the sweet and gentle flower saw this, she wept and pleaded with the hunter: 'Uncle, I beg you to spare my husband. If you need medicine, pick my flowers.' The hunter was moved by the flower's tears and consented to her request. So the brave little flower offered her own blooms to save the life of the snake—which is why the snake's pillow has been used ever since to cure convulsions.

"But even this didn't change the snake's behavior toward the little red flower. In fact, he became more brutal and vicious all the time. He knew how lovely the little flower was and was afraid that others would see her, so he wouldn't let her out in the sun, keeping her in damp marshy places where nobody else would go. If anyone praised the little flower's beauty or picked one of her blossoms, the snake would give chase and bring disaster on that person.

"As time went by, nobody would pick the snake's pillow anymore. Beautiful and lovable it may be, but it has gradually come to be forgotten."

"Is that the end?" The girl looked up, seeming dissatisfied with the way the story finished.

"That's it." The mother nodded and gave a slight sigh.

"But why didn't the little flower run away?" she asked innocently.

"Silly child, where was there to go?" With a bitter smile, the mother said pensively, "There are snakes everywhere, you know!"

"Then why was the snake beastly just to this one flower?" The girl was still curious and upset.

The mother bit her lip in the silence. Looking down, she saw that the snake's pillows were in full bloom, like stars, like dawn, like gems, red as blood, moist and sleek. . . .

After a long while she looked up. Her lips, bloodless white, trembled slightly as she spat our her answer:

"Because it has no thorns."

The Web

—1—

Clang! Clang! Clang!

"I stole the team's barley; don't be like me. . . ."

The ringing of the brass gong and the loud droning voice reverberated around the village. Step by step she made her way along the road now red in the setting sun. Her lifeless eyes showed a bewildered detachment, as if she were wondering whether this rough and shameless voice could really be hers. She halted for a moment and looked around, and when she saw that the voice was indeed coming from her own scrawny chest, she couldn't help but feel a little alarmed. Hastily she raised the mallet and struck the gleaming brass gong another hard blow.

Clang! The sound of the struck metal, reverberating around the village and trailing off to its final faint echo, underscored her words the more compellingly. People put down their rice bowls and stood in their doorways watching with relish as the thieving woman with the bedraggled hair made her way past their gates, the sound of the gong whetting their appetites. Children put down their bowls and chased after her in little groups, picking up clods of earth to throw, taunting her as they hurled them: "Toughie, Toughie, the more she's hit, the tougher she gets!"

"Toughie?" she puzzled. "Can they mean me?"

Before she had a chance to work this out, a clod landed squarely on her shoulders, hitting with a thud and bursting into pieces. Bits went down her neck, itching terribly. At last she realized that "Toughie" really did mean her. Not a good name, certainly, not even a real name, but what did that matter? Since nobody thought of her as a real person, how could she have a real name?

But she had had a fine name once. Her father and mother, who had lived by the faraway Huai River, named her Xiu, "Beautiful." No one here, where they had fled in the famines of 1960, had been able to understand her name as she pronounced it in her native dialect.

Her idle husband, Rainy, was forever beating her when he was drunk. The first time she ran for comfort to the arms of warmhearted Granny Li and cried her heart out. The second time she went down among the riverbank briars and sobbed, standing motionless for hours, watching as flock after flock of wild geese flew north. The third time he beat her she neither cried nor sulked, but giggled as Granny Li came to comfort her: "It's nothing, it doesn't matter, let him hit me. The more I'm hit, the tougher I get!" And so she came to be known as Toughie.

The day before, while everybody was having their noon rest, Toughie had stolen three pounds of barley—duck fodder—from the duck pen and had been caught in the act by Brigade Party Secretary Lai. Secretary Lai had ordered that after work today, as a public punishment for her crime, Toughie was to parade around the village.

Ignoring the jeering behind her, Toughie called out and beat the gong, then beat the gong and called out again, following her instructions to the letter. But her deadened nerves rebelled; she hazily recalled her mother and father telling her that at the time of the land reform, they had put a high hat on the landlord's head and ordered him to parade round the streets beating a gong. She also remembered how, a few years ago, the commune secretary had been paraded along this same street beating a gong. Why was it her turn now? She was puzzled and couldn't think of a reason—to think at all was a waste of time.

The descending dusk transformed everything gradually: it edged out the last slanting rays of sunlight from the roofs, then cast a dark shadow on the stream with its border of lush green bamboo, blending the dense briars and the two slender silk trees into a single hazy form. A couple of ducks, lost on their long way home, quacked forlornly in some recess of the stream.

"I stole. . . ." Toughie's voice suddenly dropped, and she choked back the rest of the sentence. Anxiously she looked up and down the road, then turned and, disregarding the route she was supposed to be taking, cut into a watermelon field beside the road.

There wasn't anything so terrifying on the road—just a crowd of schoolchildren in the distance, satchels on their backs, singing a song, and obviously just out of school. One of the schoolchildren was her only child, a little girl called Axiu, "Beauty." Beauty was thin and pale, a head shorter than other children her age, and her clothes were shabby, though cleanly washed.

Only when Toughie was certain that the children had passed and were a long way off did she relax enough to strike the gong again and resume her wailing: "I stole the team's. . . ."

She lingered over the word *stole* as if too numb to comprehend the word's shameful meaning. Yet this couldn't be completely true, or why would she be so fearful that her daughter and her classmates might see her?

"Stole . . . ," she cried, raising her lusterless eyes as if calling out to something in the darkness or straining to work out the meaning of the word. Darkness fell, obscuring the melon field and the thatched hut beside it, obscuring the village behind her with its wisps of cooking smoke. . . .

Suddenly she saw in her mind's eye the sun rising, the scorching June sun on the plains north of the Huai River, shining blindingly over an endless expanse of green crops. She was young then, gathering grasses by the roadside, so thirsty she felt her throat was on fire. She broke off a stalk of sorghum, peeled off the green skin, and chewed it like sugarcane. But before she had finished it, her thin body was grabbed by a rough hand, and another hand, big as a palm-leaf fan, walloped her bottom. She gasped, but couldn't cry out. Her mother rushed over and clung to the hand, pleading desperately, "Daddy, Daddy, she's only a child; what kind of crime has she committed for you to be hitting her so hard?"

The father growled, "If she thinks she can get away with pinching communal property when she's small, she'll be bound to steal when she grows up unless I teach her a good lesson."

Steal—the word entered her vocabulary for the first time in her simple life so full of hardship. From then on, she understood that a person shouldn't steal.

Later, when disaster struck in 1960, and starving people swarmed like locusts, her parents took her away from this familiar home, fleeing for their lives. One day when they were simply too hungry to walk, her mother collapsed by the roadside, her face waxy pale, her rubbery legs swollen thick as turnips with schistosomiasis. She knelt by her mother's side and wept. Panting for breath, her father went off somewhere and returned with a handful of sweet potatoes. As soon as she saw them she grabbed one, wiped off the soil, and held it up to her mother's mouth. Then she thought—there's no village ahead of us, no shops behind us, so where can these sweet potatoes have come from? At this her eyes widened involuntarily, and she stared at her father: "Dad, this sweet potato is. . . . "

"Eat it!" shouted her father, glowering at her.

She dared not ask more, but put her head down and gnawed ravenously at the raw vegetable, dirt, peel, and all. As she was gnawing away, suddenly tears welled up in her eyes, and she wept. Was it for hunger? Or her mother's illness? Or because her father had stolen sweet potatoes from someone else's land? She didn't know. Still she wept. Her tears were a pure spring that flowed into the stream of her life, a stream that had now become muddied.

But today she could no longer cry. Her dull eyes were two dry wells.

"I stole the team's barley; don't be like me."

Her wretched voice resounded in the lonely gloom, as if to provide a diversion for the listeners' drab lives.

She thought back to the year she was sixteen, when they came to this beautiful village by a stream. They had begged all the way, she half carrying her feverish mother, as her father wheezed with asthma.

They crowded with other refugees into a tumbledown thatched hut, the hut that was now in front of her on the melon field. Today it was completely fixed up, and the old man who guarded the melons lived there. Back then, the hut was open to the elements on three sides, and it was the coldest part of winter, when dripping water turned to ice. Her father wheezed all night, unable to lie down; her mother's forehead was burning hot. At first light, she took their battered basket and went out into the village to beg.

The road was frozen hard and very slippery. Dry wisps of grass quivered on the paths between the fields. A dog came up behind and snapped at her. She was frightened and tried to run away, but her foot slipped, and she fell heavily. She rubbed her forehead; it was all bloodied.

Children surrounded her—children didn't play mean

tricks in those days—and instructed her: "Off you go, off you go, go and beg at Rainy's house, go and beg at Rainy's house, Brother Rainy's eating dumplings in soup today."

Somehow she made it to Rainy's doorway. When she looked up, she saw that grass was growing on the roof of the squat building, the door frame was at a slant, and the house looked as if it were about to fall down. She hesitated for a moment, so the children called out for her: "Brother Rainy, do a good deed . . . give some food away . . . do a good deed. . . ."

Rainy was well known as a bachelor in the village—if he was fed, then the whole household was fed; if he locked his door, there was only his stool inside, and that wouldn't starve. Today he really was having dumplings. He had borrowed a couple of pounds of rice flour the previous evening and got up before dawn to chop meat and knead dough. At the moment she arrived, dumplings were bobbing up and down in boiling water, white and glistening, giving off an enticing aroma.

Rainy looked up and saw the girl standing in front of his door. Her small face was streaked with blood and dirt, and her dark eyes were looking down at her feet, which were bare even in winter. Somehow he was moved to compassion; he filled a bowl with dumplings and called to the girl: "Come in and eat."

When the other children heard this, they clapped their hands and jumped up and down, singing, "Rainy wants a wife! Rainy wants a wife!"

Rainy picked up a poker and brandished it threateningly at the children to frighten them away. Back in the house, he handed her the bowl of dumplings, but she wouldn't eat, and her tears splashed into the bowl. When he asked her why, she told him about her sick parents in the thatched hut.

Rainy said no more, but tipped the dumplings into his washbasin, added a few more ladlefuls, then told her to take the dumplings to her parents.

Because of that basin of dumplings, her parents knelt at Rainy's feet and begged him to keep their unfortunate daughter. Rainy was by then already in his thirties, but since he was lazy and greedy, none of the local girls were prepared to take him on. As he looked at this little beggar girl, he saw that with her oval face freshly washed, she was quite pretty, and her big dark eyes were gentle and beautiful. He was delighted beyond his hopes—how could he refuse?

The girl hid behind her mother's back, terrified at the prospect of leaving her parents and living her whole life with this sallow-faced stranger.

"Dad, don't cast your daughter away, please, please!" she sobbed.

Her father clouted her: "Don't be stupid: do you want to die with us?"

That evening, her father sent her to Rainy's house to borrow some matches. Rainy barred the door and kept her inside all night. Next morning she rushed round to the thatched hut, threw herself on her mother, and wept: "Ma, who's going to fetch water for you? Who's going to massage Dad's back? . . ."

Her mother wiped her tears with the edge of her jacket: "Child, don't blame your father. We just can't bear to watch you starving to death with us. If you marry and stay where there's food to eat, then I can die content."

So she was married to Rainy. The day they married, the government issued an order that all refugees were to be sent back to their own villages. That night as she lay next to Rainy, she told him that somehow they must get hold of some grain for her parents to take home. Rainy gritted his teeth: "Okay, they can have the hundred pounds of rice we were allocated yesterday. Since we're staying here, we should be able to come up with something."

Her father took the grain to market to exchange it for money and grain coupons, which would be easier to carry. She waited all day, but her parents didn't come back to the thatched hut. She became worried and ran all the way to the market to look for them. When she got there, she found her mother collapsed on the ground, her swollen legs splayed out behind her, convulsed with tears, and her father pleading on his knees. The market supervisor had accused them of profiteering and confiscated their grain.

—3—

Had her mother died? Had her father got back home alive? Toughie's dull, slow eyes flickered for a moment as the memories flooded back.

She would never forget the man with the stubbly beard who confiscated their grain, his expressionless face and cold stare. Snatching away the grain, he had snatched away the lives of her mother and father. Why wasn't it him parading along the street? Why hadn't he been made to do it?

Clang!

She hit the gong hard, but the sound was still much weaker than it had been when she started. The children behind harangued her, complaining that she wasn't doing it properly. So she shouted at the top of her voice: "I stole the team's barley. . . ."

Dimly she returned to that day in 1960, twelve years before. When she returned sobbing and wailing from the market, Rainy took his fury out on her: "It's all your fault, a hundred pounds of rice down the drain."

She wept as if she were crying her life away, as Rainy stormed out to get a drink. Late at night when he came staggering drunkenly home, he was carrying a fat duck.

She trembled with fright. "Wh—— . . . where did you get that from? We may be poor, but we . . . we mustn't do anything immoral."

"Immoral?" Rainy sneered, "It's immoral when food is stuck in front of your face and you don't eat it! I didn't set out to steal it; I just picked it up in the reeds by the river."

"Picked it up?" she echoed, "That must be somebody's duck that's got lost. Take it back!"

"You talk too much," said Rainy as he wrung the duck's neck. "Boil some water, and pluck it, quickly!"

"It's stolen, stolen," she thought as she boiled the water. A bitter realization gnawed at her—she was married to a thief!

Early the next morning an old woman stormed around the village complaining that someone had made off with her duck and saying that she hoped the thief would come to a bad end and die childless. The girl panicked and rushed out to get rid of the feathers. But as luck would have it, someone spotted her, and the news spread like wildfire through the village.

"Thieving bitch," accused their eastern neighbor's wife behind her back.

"Pilferer," sneered their western neighbor's mother-in-law, narrowing her eyes.

Everyone knew she wasn't to be trusted and guarded their property from her. Wherever she went, it was like a plague passing by. Even diapers hung out to dry were whisked inside for fear she might steal them.

—4—

When her daughter was born the following year, the team refused to recognize the mother and daughter because they hadn't completed the formalities required for marriage and registering a transfer of household; moreover, they hadn't given the team leader a present. Without household registration there was no allocation of grain, and they were worse off than ever.

One evening, Rainy threw a bag at her feet and said, "Everyone says you're a thief, and they'll say it if you steal or not. There are some beans in the plot to the west that look as if they're growing well. Go get some."

She bowed her head silently, bent down to pick up the bag, and crept into the blackness outside.

Moonlight gleamed through the drifting clouds, and the fragrance of alfalfa wafted on the evening breeze. Trembling, she sneaked into the bean plot behind the team's storehouse. It was black as a bottomless lake.

As her feet stepped on leaves covered with frost and her fingers brushed the plump furry pods, a fit of trembling overcame her. She fought with herself, struggling to pluck a bean pod, but just couldn't do it. Finally her legs went limp, and she slumped to her knees.

"Dad, Ma!" She closed her eyes for shame in the darkness.

She heard something. It was very soft, the sound of footsteps and turning wheels. If she hadn't been so alert, the sound might have dissolved in the clear breeze and the full night air. But at that moment it rang like thunder in Toughie's sensitive ear. She thought it was someone coming for her, someone who must have been following her. . . .

"I'm going to get caught," she thought, cowering like a frightened rabbit. She was like an animal cornered by a hunter.

But after quite a while, when no one had come into the bean plot, she plucked up the courage to part the dense foliage and steal a glimpse into the moonlight. Incredible! She almost gasped out loud at what she saw. The door of the storehouse was open, and Team Leader Lai Changyou came tiptoeing out with a bulging grain sack on his shoulder, which he lowered onto his bicycle seat and secured with a rope.

What was the team leader doing taking grain in the middle of the night? Hadn't he said a few days before that the team was losing grain and asked the authorities to investigate? Surely it couldn't be Team Leader Lai himself that was. . . .

Toughie shivered at the thought. She felt that she couldn't stay where she was. She had to get away, or at least hide herself deeper in the bean plot. But her movements were too flustered, and with the first step she tripped over a bean creeper, making a terrible noise.

Before she could get to her feet, a flashlight shone in her face.

"Oh, Team . . . Team Leader Lai!" she cried, shaking with fear.

"So, caught red-handed " Team Leader Lai stooped to pick up her bag. "What's this then?"

"I didn't, I didn't. . . ." She was trembling so much she couldn't finish.

Team Leader Lai didn't say another word, but narrowed his eyes and kept his flashlight trained on her—trained on her face, which, though pale, hadn't lost its beauty, trained on her firm young breasts.

"Please, Team Leader, I beg you!" She was still shaking.

"Maybe I will let you off this once," he said, tossing his flashlight aside.

The next moment, she was being forced down by the man's powerful hands into the dense greenery of the bean plot. . . .

—5—

Ah, the broad beans, firm ripe pods shaded by lush green leaves, fragrant in the evening breeze. How could she ever have come here again? She didn't know.

As she stood on the plot where she had lost her honor, a wave of emotion welled up in her numbed heart.

She remembered that for several days after her rape by Team Leader Lai, she had stood dumbly by the stream behind the bamboo grove, watching the rich scarlet blossoms of the silk tree as they dropped one by one into the water. The thought came to her that she could throw herself in too, and float with the red blossoms into another world. In that world, she would be reunited with her parents, she wouldn't be insulted or abused. . . .

But she couldn't, she couldn't! There was another part of her life that she couldn't throw away—she had a baby daughter!

The evening breeze dried the sweat on her clothing, and she felt comforted. She bent down to look at the clumps of late-flowering beans, pink flowers each with a pair of dark eyes in the middle. How spirited they were, how full of life! What were they like? Yes, they were like her daughter Beauty's shining black eyes.

Beauty had smiled from birth. She had thin lips, and regular white teeth like pearls, and the clearly defined features typical of girls from north of the Huai. Ah, that such flesh should have come from her own body!

Beauty shone a ray of sunlight into her life. Her husband's beatings, the villagers' insults, her humiliation by the team leader . . . she could stand them all. When choosing a name for the girl, she had called her Beauty because she remembered that her own parents had called her Beautiful and taught her always to be honest and trustworthy. . . .

She had long since ceased to be her parents' Beautiful, but she felt that her daughter deserved a new life, a new future. So on the day Beauty reached the age of seven, she took her to the village primary school. The poor child was so frail that she looked two years younger. There just wasn't enough for her to eat.

Even though she had lost her honor, even though everyone regarded her as a thieving bitch, she had to survive for her daughter's sake. She had no choice but to steal beans or make off with a watermelon—she really was a thief now. But these things never reached her daughter's mouth; Rainy was as bad as ever, grabbing whatever was good to eat, finishing it up before the night was out—in his own words, even a rat couldn't get anything out of him. When a theft was discovered, he would push his wife to the doorway and thrash her, bawling at her as the blows descended: "I'll teach you to steal! I'll teach you!" loud enough for all the village to hear.

"Rainy's beating that thieving bitch again!" the village men would comment.

"She doesn't mind, though. She said it herself: the more she's beaten, the tougher she gets," sniggered the women.

But Granny Li, who wiped Toughie's tears, would always say: "She must have sinned in a past life. Now she has to live with a lout like that and raise the child too—it's hard on her!"

Toughie really did keep on getting tougher—even though she lived on husks and weeds, though she became thin and sallow, there wasn't a woman in the village to match her for energy. Morning and night she cut wild grasses and dug for yams, scratching round like a mother hen to feed her daughter, Beauty.

By day she looked after the ducks in the village duck pond, where Secretary Lai (he had risen from team leader to brigade Party secretary) would come from time to time. Not for her, of course—she could no longer be described as beautiful, with her wrinkled face and her body shriveled like a dried eggplant. When Secretary Lai caught a glimpse of her, even from a distance, he would frown.

He came to fetch duck eggs. He would come up with various reasons for taking them, filling his basket with the biggest and freshest eggs and taking them home. They were for himself and to offer to his superiors, commune and county officials. Sometimes he would get Toughie to pack them or pick out the best for him.

She didn't know whether what Secretary Lai was doing counted as "stealing"; the question never occurred to her. But as she packed the eggs for him, the image of her daughter's pale thin face flashed through her mind.

—6—

Beauty was a clever child, always at the top of her class. In the school examination, she had finished second. The teacher who had supervised the exam said sympathetically that if it hadn't been for her fainting and being unable to finish the last part of the paper, she'd certainly have come in first.

The mother knew perfectly well what had made Beauty ill. The girl was starving! If only Beauty had eaten a duck egg every day, she would certainly not have fainted in the exam room. But the child understood well enough how things were—every time one of their hens or ducks laid, Rainy would grab the egg and boil it to eat when he had a drink, and she would stand by and watch, silent and uncomplaining. Every morning she would eat only a bowl of vegetable gruel before going to school.

But for the last few days, Beauty hadn't even had gruel to eat. How could her mother let her go to school on an empty stomach? There was nothing else for it—she took some scoops of barley from the tub of duck feed and hid it, intending to take it home and boil it up as a meal for her daughter. However, Secretary Lai arrived unexpectedly at the duck pen to get his basket filled with eggs, and he noticed straightaway that Toughie's cracked jar was full of barley. He smashed the jar, spilling the golden grain on the floor, and swore at Toughie for being a habitual thief.

When Toughie saw that Secretary Lai had smashed her jar, she seemed to lose control. She fell to her knees, scratching up the grains of barley, almost knocking her head on his feet: "Please, Secretary Lai, I beg you, be merciful, my daughter Beauty has nothing to eat. . . . "

Secretary Lai snorted: "Thieving woman, this time I won't let you off!"

"I beg you, I beg you!" Toughie fell at Secretary Lai's feet and pleaded desperately with him.

"No chance!" said Secretary Lai decisively. "I'm going to fine you two hundred pounds of grain. If I didn't and people found out, then petty thieves like you would pinch everything in the duck pen in no time!"

"Fine me grain . . . thief?" To Toughie, it seemed like a strange voice coming from far away. She stopped pleading and looked up slowly, staring at Secretary Lai, sizing up his pock-marked face, sizing up the basket filled to the brim with eggs. Then she thought of all the baskets of duck eggs that Secretary Lai had taken away from the duck pen, the bulging sack of grain he had taken from the village granary. . . . Suddenly she sprang up, her pupils dilated, her dull eyes suddenly furious as they fixed on Secretary Lai: "I'm a petty thief all right . . . but you took away the team's grain in the middle of the night, you carried off baskets of eggs from the duck pen to eat at home . . . isn't that stealing too? What you've stolen is too much to be counted. If you say I'm a petty thief, then you're a big thief!"

Toughie felt a certain sense of relief that she had at last, after so many years, stood up to Secretary Lai. But he thought she had gone crazy. He beat her up and then gave the order that she was to parade the streets in public view.

"I stole the team's barley. . . ," she called out, and looked up at the sky, as if she had never before studied its colors. For the first time she saw that the sky at dusk could be inky black, yet at the edges of that blackness appeared the pink radiance of sunset clouds, and above that the boundless gray of the sky.

Strange, how could the same sky be so pink, so gray, so black? The world was simply unfathomable.

The gray reminded her of the shell of a duck egg. Yes, duck eggs, grayish-white like fat pearls, packed one after another into Secretary Lai's basket. . . .

Maybe she shouldn't have filled her jar with duck feed. Maybe she should have filled a basket with duck eggs instead.

Maybe. . . .

Duck eggs, baskets, the colors of the sky . . . wasn't theft when Secretary Lai did it. . . .

Clang! She struck the gong again. "I stole the team's barley; don't be like me."

"Toughie, the more she's hit, the tougher she gets!" Clods of earth rained down on her back.

Clang! She struck the gong again and called out unthinkingly: "Don't be like me. If you're going to steal, don't steal duck feed. Fill a basket with eggs, fill a sack with grain!"

Whoever would have thought that these wild words from a low thieving woman would carry like a whirlwind into every corner of the village? People sitting out with their dinner to watch the fun looked in dismay at one another, forgetting to swallow the food in their mouths. They exchanged looks of amazement and understanding; those with chopsticks in midair were suddenly unable to move. Secretary Lai hurled down his wineglass and stormed out of his house, the faint white pockmarks on his face turning a dark gray. Granny Li recited the name of the Buddha and hobbled out to restrain the hurtful children. Parents put on their most authoritative voices: "Little Root! Come here and get your dinner, you little bastard!" "Brightie, get back here right now, and lock up the duck pen!"

The children didn't understand what was going on, but they got even more excited because their parents were yelling at them. They picked up more clods of dripping mud and jumped up and down, shouting: "Toughie, Toughie. . . ."

At the very instant one of the children was about to throw his mud pie, Granny Li grabbed him from behind, and the mud pie flew off target, landing with a smack on Secretary Lai's neck.

". . . the more she's hit, the tougher she gets!"

The pure voices of the children rang out in the deepening gloom.

—8—

When she heard that her mother had lost her mind during her parade through the village, that she had been tied up by the village militia and locked in the team's woodshed, Beauty rushed over.

The unfeeling blackness swallowed everything. The two silk trees on either side of the river, so beautiful by day, now cast dark shadows like gravestones on the surface of the water. A tall gingko tree towered like a ghost in the open field, the patch of rape seed was dark as a bottomless pool, and there was whispering in the bamboo groves. All this would have been terrifying for most eleven-year-olds, but Beauty was quite unafraid, her frail body weighed down with grief and shame.

Here I am doing so well at school, and Ma does something awful like this, she thought. Her face burned with shame, and she wanted the darkness to swallow her up.

But when she thought of how loving her mother had always been to her, how much hardship her mother had endured to send her to school, tears poured down from her eyes, soaking her Young Pioneers red scarf, tears that washed the shame from Beauty's heart and turned it to sympathy and love for her mother.

It was late in the night when she felt her way into the woodshed, cut her mother's bonds, and half dragged, half carried her home.

Toughie was awakened by the sound of sobbing, and when she opened her eyes, she was in her own bed, her daughter watching over her.

In her confused state, she thought that this was not her daughter, this was herself as a child, crying at her mother's bedside.

"Mama!" That was certainly her daughter's clear voice, far away yet near at hand. She opened her eyes, staring into her daughter's tear-stained face. She saw her own past in her daughter and her daughter's future in herself. Her eyes suddenly lit up, and she struggled to a sitting position, then leaned forward and with trembling hands felt under the bed.

"Mama, what do you want? I'll get it for you!" wailed Beauty in alarm.

Her mother paid her no attention, just kept feeling around, and after some time brought out a small bottle. She clasped Beauty to her breast and ran her fingers through the girl's coarse hair.

"Ma!" Beauty's small body trembled slightly, as though she had guessed her mother's intention. Her mother slowly pulled the stopper out of the bottle and said: "Beauty, darling, let's both drink it."

Beauty looked at the label that read *insecticide* and collapsed to her knees, shaking her mother's body and screaming: "Please Ma, I don't want to die, I want to live. . . . I was top in the arithmetic test . . . please, Ma, please. . . ."

As Beauty wrenched the bottle away, Toughie moaned and fainted.

Thereafter, Toughie lapsed in and out of consciousness. Beauty stayed by her mother's side and wept, hardly noticing as her classmates came to show her the results of the exams, in all of which she had scored As, and to give her a prize certificate.

Once when Toughie recovered consciousness, it seemed that she had thought of something while she was comatose; gasping, she raised herself up and pointed to the corner of the room.

Beauty followed the direction of her finger and found a boiled egg hidden under a pile of grass and twigs. She realized that her mother had hidden it there for her. She held the egg to her heart, and her tears splashed down.

—9—

On the flaking whitewashed wall, a spider was busy.

It sauntered like a scholar-official in his shiny black gown, slender legs moving unhurriedly. On the drab, dusty wall of this sad cold room, bare of furniture, it wove a web. Solemnly, the spider took control of the place.

At every point on its slow journey it released a fine thread. One end was anchored to bare gray brick, the other to Beauty's certificate. The web quivered, but did not break.

Toughie woke and, seeing the cobweb on her daughter's certificate, thought she would brush it off, squash this infuriating spider. But it required a tremendous effort to move, and she just couldn't raise her hand. She could only watch as the spider wove its web.

The web, huge and close-meshed, filled one corner of the shabby room and finally covered Beauty's certificate. Toughie felt an anxiety, an ominous premonition.

Why this premonition? She forced herself to open her eyes and concentrate, but she couldn't think of a reason. Then she caught sight of a small fly with bright green wings flying to and fro, a pretty little thing. Her eyes followed the fly everywhere. It flew upward and was snared in the spider's web in the corner of the room. Struggle as it might, it was held fast in the web and couldn't get free. The spider scuttled over to the little green fly and sprang on it, forcing itself down on the fly's body and devouring it greedily.

Gradually the spider's stomach swelled, and the fly became an empty shell hanging from the web.

One, another, a third . . . the empty shells of innumerable small flies hung from the web. No wonder the spider looked so at ease, like a bodhisattva that controls all it surveys.

In the darkness, Toughie thought that she was caught in a great web, that the spider's mouth was jabbing at her flesh, sucking at her, sucking, until finally her body was an empty shell like those of the flies hanging from the close-meshed and unyielding web.

"Mama, Mama . . . ," she heard Beauty's frantic call.

"Beauty's Ma, Beauty's Ma . . . ," came the voice of the kindly Granny Li.

Flap-Eared Hulk and His Bobtail Dog

—1—

The production team leader came back from a meeting at brigade headquarters with a litter of rabbits. He went through the village, telling everyone that these were newly imported West German angora rabbits, and trying to persuade people to buy them. He told them that three ounces of fur could be clipped from each adult four times a year, and as the fur was worth twenty yuan a pound, it would clearly be possible to make over twenty yuan per rabbit per year. It followed that ten rabbits would bring in more than two hundred a year, on top of which their owners would be awarded extra cloth and grain coupons. Those who were bold enough to raise a few dozen or even a hundred rabbits could make a fortune! And because the state was encouraging peasants to raise rabbits as part of the new policy of developing sideline enterprises, not only were the rabbits available at below-market price, only ten yuan a pair, but they also came with a free manual on how to look after them.

The strange thing was that, despite these incentives, there were no buyers. The problem was that nobody could actually see the wonderful benefits the rabbits would bring, but the money they had to shell out was all too real. Old-timers shook their heads and clucked their tongues: "Pricey, too pricey. They cost too much!" And they had a point! Even in the famine years of the early sixties, when the price of an egg had risen to fifty cents, baby rabbits had only cost two yuan a pair. Then, when you fattened them up, they only fetched five yuan, less than you could get for a chicken. Now, with eggs ten cents apiece, these rabbits cost ten yuan a pair! You'd have to be crazy to think this was a good deal.

The team leader was young and forceful and would not accept such woolly thinking. He countered, "Those rabbits you're talking about were bred for meat, and these are fur-bearing. You wouldn't expect them to cost the same, would you?"

It wasn't that anyone was questioning the team leader's assertions. These people weren't fools—they could figure out for themselves that if you really could clip the rabbits once a quarter, and if a pound of the fur would fetch twenty yuan, then the rabbits would be good value at fifty the pair, let alone ten! Here's how: You buy a breeding pair and do the first clipping in three months. One cut recoups the investment, and, seeing that they're rabbits, they're reproducing all the time, so you could be building yourself a mansion in three years! Added to which, rabbits are less bother than pigs since they're cleaner and don't eat as much. A child could pick all the food the rabbits would need on the way home from school. A deal as good as this was like food dropping from heaven!

If it really was such a good deal, it stood to reason that people ought to have been falling over each other to get in on it. So why did the team leader have to tramp around talking till his mouth was dry and his head was aching? The villagers all reasoned that in today's world you have to be well connected to get anything worth having, and even then there's no guarantee that you can actually buy it. So why the sales pitch? If something needs a sales pitch, it's obviously hard to sell, and if it's hard to sell, how can it be any good? Given this way of thinking, everyone steered clear of the deal as if it were a serpent disguised as a beauty. The villagers resisted the seductive charms of a high return on investment, dwelling instead on the unseen pitfalls that might lie in their path. What if you couldn't actually shear any fur off them? What if government buyers stopped accepting rabbit fur? What if people were suddenly forbidden to keep rabbits at all? . . .

Such misgivings were by no means uncalled for—there was a precedent for each one of them. In the past there had been calls to develop sideline enterprises, followed by campaigns to "cut off the tails of capitalism"; there was the time the pharmacy had been buying ground beetles and then abruptly stopped taking them; and . . . well, another important consideration was that nobody had ever seen these foreign rabbits before, so nobody had any idea if there was any difference between these rabbits and the indigenous Chinese variety. Sure, these cuddly little snowballs were cute, but place them beside any common local rabbit, and they wouldn't seem all that special. What if they weren't really foreign fur-bearing rabbits but just some Chinese variety?

The team leader was able to set them straight on this matter at least—the state would not, of course, deceive the people, so if they were supposed to be foreign rabbits, there could be no mistake about it. They were foreign rabbits.

Okay, so they're foreign rabbits. Who do we know who's ever raised them? Everyone knows that Chinese people can live on rice gruel but foreigners need dairy products—it's always possible that foreign rabbits might have similarly refined tastes. If not, why do you need a manual to look after them? There were people who'd been raising rabbits all their lives and couldn't read a single character, and now they were expected to work their way through some vast tome. Wasn't this like teaching old dogs new tricks and making them look silly in the process? And then you might put out money for these dainty little creatures and have them end up dying on you if you didn't treat them right, which would truly "exhaust the people and break the bank."

That's typical of the way people's minds work—they won't weave nets till they see fish, and by then it's too late.

But even though they didn't want to weave nets themselves, they all kept their eyes wide open to see whether anyone else would give net weaving a try. As long as everyone refused to buy, they could all rest easy and sleep well. But if anyone were rash enough to take the plunge and buy a pair, that would set everyone else's hearts pounding. Should they get weaving themselves? Otherwise they might be left watching as someone else hauled in the catch, and wouldn't that leave a bad taste in the mouth!

Everyone must have reckoned the same way; after two days, nobody had bought any. Schoolchildren fell for the baby rabbits as soon as they set eyes on them. They would come along in little groups after school with fresh shoots of tender grass, and hop up and down squealing with glee at the rabbits, their innocent eyes gleaming with fierce longing. The team leader would only have had to nod his head, and they would willingly have brought out their most treasured possessions to exchange for a baby rabbit. The pure white fur, the nimble hopping, the warm softness in the hand, all delighted the little children beyond belief. The pity of it was that the children had no money, and even the most doting of parents weren't going to give in to their pleading.

On the third day a big fellow in his thirties showed up as proud as could be with over thirty yuan in his pocket to buy rabbits. The news spread like wildfire, causing general dismay. But when the identity of the buyer became known, everyone heaved a sigh of relief: "Oh, that's okay. It's only him!" And with that, everything went back to normal.

Now why should it be that *him* buying rabbits didn't bother people, still less make them feel threatened?

—2—

There's a long story behind it.

He was called Hulk, and, true to his name, every part of him was hulking. Big head, big feet, big nose, big eyes. And biggest of all, his fleshy protruding ears. No doubt his size had been apparent when he was still a toddler, which would account for his parents' choice of a name for him.

The year Hulk turned sixteen was one of great hardship for the nation. One day his mother told him to take an old goat to market, and to his delight he was able to trade it for a sack of flour. As he was walking back with the sack over his shoulder, he saw someone sitting by the road holding a newborn puppy, its eyes just barely open. With its yellow body, little red mouth, and timid staring eyes, the puppy was truly adorable. Hulk went over and struck up a conversation, then asked rather too enthusiastically if the dog was for sale.

The owner saw how keen he was to buy and launched forth in florid praise of the animal. He said that it was an authentic hunting dog and that when it grew up it would be able to retrieve birds from the sky, hares from the ground and badgers from their setts. The way he talked, it seemed the dog would be a match for tigers and wolves as well if there had only been some around for it to chase.

Hulk listened with increasing yearning. He loved to hunt and had always wanted a hunting dog. When he got back home, there was no trace of the sack of flour. In its place was an inedible little puppy.

His mother nearly tore his ears off over that dog. Still, she managed to get boy and dog through the hard times by gleaning waterweeds and grinding their roots into a coarse flour, before abandoning them all too soon by her early death.

Orphaned he may have been, but Hulk never felt particularly lonely, since his hunting dog had now grown up. One sunny day he took the dog out on a hunting trip. "In and kill!" he ordered her down a badger sett. The dog didn't move a muscle, let alone go down the hole. She was a useless mongrel.

Hulk felt neither discouraged nor resentful. Instead he decided he would mate his mongrel to a genuine hunting dog from another village. She bore a single pup.

Just as loving parents will sometimes deliberately pick an inauspicious name for a child to protect it from misfortune, so Hulk, hoping for a valiant hunting dog, gave it the unpromising name Lazybones.

Lazybones lived up to expectations. He grew up bold and pugnacious and provided his master with game to eat and sell.

Hulk's luck didn't last. All too soon there came the campaign to "cut off the tails of capitalism." His gun was confiscated at a public meeting, and such prestige as he had won as an exemplary poor peasant turned into disgrace. What caused him the greatest grief was the team leader's order that he kill his dog in full view of everyone.

To kill Lazybones would be like destroying himself. The usually phlegmatic Hulk was on the verge of tears. In his despair he seized the cleaver and brought it down with a whack, cutting off the dog's tail. Lazybones squealed in agony, his severed tail sticky with blood. His face ashen, Hulk threw the cleaver aside and stammered: "There's the tail, the tail of capitalism, and I cut . . . I cut it right off!"

The brigade Party secretary was taken aback for a moment, but then he nodded his head: "Hm, not bad, your attitude is resolute."

So that crisis subsided. Hulk's disposition remained unchanged, however, and it wasn't long before he came up with a moneymaking scheme—this time raising ground beetles, which the pharmacy was buying to make into a traditional medicine. With a certain amount of hard work, a good return on the initial investment was all but guaranteed.

By that time he was no longer the happy-go-lucky bachelor he had once been, but a married man with a young son. His nearest and dearest hit the roof when he went to her for money to buy beetle eggs: "Haven't you got yourself into enough trouble already without this?" His wife's word was law, so of course he didn't dare mention it again.

After a while, the tail cutters had their own tails docked—the Gang of Four was overthrown! Now more and more people got into the ground-beetle business, and word got around that there were families who had built grand two-story houses on the proceeds. Timidly Hulk passed this news on to his wife, and she let herself be persuaded by him—in fact she was herself infected with the current craze for buying ground-beetle eggs. So she gave him the money.

The price of the beetle eggs was going up every day. From the twenty yuan a pound they had been when Hulk first suggested the idea to his wife, they went up to fifty, and by the time she actually handed over the money, they were selling for a hundred and were in short supply. He was hard-pressed to find someone to buy a pound of the eggs on his behalf.

To his dismay, half the eggs he bought didn't hatch. Hulk asked around and discovered that those eggs that didn't hatch had been boiled. The vendor suspected that anyone who bought the eggs was going to breed the beetles. As the saying goes, "there's value in rarity," and too much proliferation was likely to drive the price down. Even if the price remained stable, there would be more people cashing in on the bonanza, and that was a prospect he didn't relish. So he hit on a plan that would allow him to make a pile of money and stop anyone cutting in on his profits: boil some of the eggs, and mix them in with the live ones fifty-fifty. The result was that Hulk had paid double for his live eggs.

Fortunately Hulk cared for the eggs conscientiously, grateful at least that half of them had been all right, and within a couple of weeks a fine crop of glossy black beetles had hatched.

He kept them in a series of little tanks he had made from cement and bricks.

Of course bugs are just bugs, and you can't get as fond of them as you can of more cuddly creatures. But when Hulk looked at those little creepie-crawlies in their tanks, he saw new hope. "Calm down, Lazybones," he told the restless dog beside him. "When I sell these beetles, I'm going to go out and buy a hunting rifle, even better than the one they took away. Then you can show me what you're made of." Lazybones couldn't wag his tail as he once had, but he held his head high and barked excitedly.

When the time came, Hulk killed and dried his beetles, packed them in a basket, and took them to the pharmacy. But when he got there, he saw a sign on the door announcing that they weren't buying any more beetles. If you have a chicken, a duck, or a sheep and you can't sell it, at least you can kill and eat it, but what possible use were a pile of shriveled black bugs?

He hadn't a clue what to do with them. But however useless they might be, he couldn't just toss them away.

He walked dejectedly round and round the pharmacy until he came to a halt before a blackboard with smudged and faded writing on it. It was an announcement from a year or so before, when the beetle trade had been at its peak. With his three years of schooling and some good guesswork he gathered that it was an article about the uses of the beetles. It seemed that they could be made into a medicine for knitting broken bones.

This discovery was a real thrill. If he couldn't sell his beetles, he might as well try to make some of the medicine himself, so he decided he would take the beetles back home. First, however, he might as well take a stroll and feast his eyes on the appetizing delights that the town had to offer. There were so many good things to eat along the streets: savory dumplings with soup fillings, spareribs embedded in New Year's cake, fresh meat dumplings in broth, doughnut sticks, sticky-rice cakes, and onion flapjacks. And then there were the sweet things: fermented rice cakes, sweet dumplings, sugar cakes, sesame balls . . . everything you could possibly want! Hulk had not been out for a meal on his own since his marriage, and his plan was not to fill his belly but to feast his eyes. After weaving his way through the streets his thoughts turned to his wife and child. Since they had missed this delicious display, he would have to find a way to make it up to them. So, fishing out the few yuan he had in his pocket, he bought a pound of meat and two pounds of dumpling wrappers. He planned to go home at noon and make a meal of meat dumplings, dumplings with no vegetable mixed in to stretch the filling. Though he hadn't been able to buy a hunting rifle, the prospect of those dumplings filled his stride with strength and purpose.

When he got home, his wife was just taking out the pan to cook some vegetables. When she heard his story, she was apoplectic, hammering the pan with her spatula and screaming, "Useless bastard, I told you not to buy them, but you still had to have your own way. So what did you think you were bringing them back here for? You expect me to cook them for you?"

"Pack them in a box, and we'll keep them." Hulk scratched his head and grinned fatuously. "They're good medicine for knitting bones. If someone falls over and breaks a leg, we can treat him right here."

"Just my luck to be saddled with a loser like you!" His wife glowered at him. "When you break a leg, you can boil up the medicine yourself!"

"Okay, good idea!" Hulk rubbed his nose inattentively. When he saw his wife preparing to serve squash and potato soup, he wanted to help her, but he wasn't sure what to do. Suddenly he remembered the meat and wrappers he had bought. He brought them out as if he were presenting a valuable gift.

At the smell of the meat, Lazybones materialized, frisking and leaping around his master. Hulk's face lit up when he saw his precious bobtail dog. The dog cozied up to Hulk for a while; then, in an attempt to be evenhanded with his owners, he bounded over to his mistress and licked her foot at precisely the moment she was taking bowls of hot soup over to the table. She tripped over him, and a bowl slipped out of her hand. The scalding broth splashed her, making her gasp with the pain. When she saw that it was that bloody dog that had tripped her, it just added fat to the flames. She grabbed a carrying pole and beat the dog savagely. Poor Lazybones squealed in agony as he fell to the ground. He lay there trembling, unable to get up. Hulk felt the pain as if it were himself who was taking the beating. He launched himself forward to embrace the dog. "Are you hurt, darling?" he asked tearfully. Lazybones just shook convulsively, one hind leg hanging limply behind him.

The stolid Hulk saw red. He raised a huge hand and took a swing at his wife: "I'll give you some of your own medicine!" It was the first time he had ever struck her.

There was no way Hulk's wife was going to stand for that. Aying hid her face in her hands and started to howl.

After a first bout of wailing, she peeped out between her fingers to see Hulk ministering to the dog and taking no notice of her, so she collapsed in tears on the quilt. Their son joined in his mother's crying, and for the rest of the day there was no fire in Hulk's kitchen.

His father-in-law heard the news and came round that evening. Aying was lying on the bed with her head covered as Hulk worked the bellows to get the fire going and brew up the ground-beetle medicine.

"What's the matter, Aying?" asked her father, his hand on her forehead.

"He beat me . . . he hurt me!" she sniffed.

"Honestly? Where are you hurt? Let Daddy see," said her father earnestly.

Aying held onto the quilt for dear life and wouldn't let him look. In fact, though Hulk did have huge hands, he had only given her a light tap, leaving no marks at all. The old man saw how things were but didn't want to make her look bad. He chuckled, "Aying, cursing and beating can be signs of affection, you know. Look how kind you husband is, making medicine for you."

At the mention of the medicine, Aying jerked upright in bed, pointed a trembling finger at Hulk, and hissed through clenched teeth, "Him, make medicine for me? That's for his dog! I'm not worth as much as a dog to him! I . . . I want a divorce. I demand divorce!"

"Divorce, eh? Haha, divorce!" The old man chuckled and twiddled with his whiskers. There was no way of knowing what was in his mind.

Hulk stood to one side, pale and anxious. It was true what his wife had said about the concoction being for the dog. After all, Lazybones was the one with the broken leg. Since he didn't have anything to say for himself, he bowed his head and listened to his wife's tearful accusations. Sniveling, she recounted all Hulk's speculations in failed enterprises and the wasted money and effort that had resulted. The old man listened and nodded. Hulk's heart sank lower and lower, then jumped up into his throat as his father-in-law gave a final profound and forceful nod. "Is that all, Aying?"

"That's all!" she answered petulantly.

Hulk felt a chill run through his whole body. He clasped Lazybones tightly, as if the dog's warmth were all that prevented him from turning to ice.

"What I recommend, daughter, is that you agree to let bygones be bygones. You weren't the only ones to lose money on the ground beetles. Take the long view—power and wealth are ordained by the heavens; a pauper won't be poor forever, nor a rich man always wealthy. . . ." The old man droned on, still stroking his whiskers.

Hulk hadn't dared hope for this from his father-in-law. Relief loosened his tongue. "You're right, Dad. Everyone's destiny is decided by his own little patch of heaven."

His wife's eyes bulged furiously: "Divorce!" she hissed again. She wasn't going down without a fight. The old man gave her a kindly look. "That's right," he said, "Hulk was wrong to hit you, and it was wrong of him to speculate the way he did. I'm going to draft a contract for the two of you. Hulk, you have to promise. . . ."

"I promise!" Hulk nodded frantically, jerking his head up and down like a chicken pecking grain.

". . . You have to promise that you will desist from perpetrating suchlike offenses." The old man was a retired schoolteacher and given to rhetorical flourishes. "Should you so transgress hereafter," he continued sententiously, "in such an eventuality, divorce would ensue." Whereupon he drew a worn fountain pen from his jacket and a cigarette package from his trousers. Shaking off the shreds of tobacco, he began to write. The old man might have been forced into retirement after twenty years of teaching, but his literary prowess was undiminished. He had the "contract" drawn up in short order, then read out the contents and instructed his son-in-law to append his signature. Hulk grasped the pen as if it were a shovel and inscribed a large and shaky *Hulk*.

The old man tucked the "contract" into his jacket and marched out. Aying got out of bed, cut the meat, and made dumplings. The boy held the dog while Hulk fed it the ground-beetle medicine. Peace and contentment returned to the house.

The threat of divorce subsided. Lazybones' leg quickly healed, thanks to his master's ministrations, and he was soon bounding through the fields near their home again.

The return of Hulk's sense of well-being made him positively garrulous. He would tell everyone he met of the efficacy of the ground-beetle cure. His listeners would all snigger to each other: "That guy Hulk, raising ground beetles to treat a dog's leg." The joke got around until it became a regular part of village folk wisdom. It was all because of this aphorism and the story behind it that when it became known that Hulk was the one buying the rabbits, there was no more interest shown than there was in schoolchildren wanting them. The poor guy wasn't any smarter than a kid anyway.

When the excited Hulk took his money round to the team leader's house, the team leader just looked disbelievingly at him: "Why didn't you come before? What held you up?" The team leader had seen that nobody was buying and taken all the rabbits back to the husbandry station. For all his fine talk, he hadn't had the nerve to buy any either.

Hulk had actually made up his mind to buy three days earlier but hadn't been able to pry the money out of his wife. It was only today that he'd got his hands on the forty yuan, though naturally he couldn't let the team leader know that.

"If you're so set on buying, go to the breeding station yourself and pick them up there," said the team leader. "There's lots to choose from."

—3—

Hulk left the team leader's house, called his dog, and set off without delay for the county town.

Everything went according to plan. He packed his new rabbits into a basket and hoisted it onto his back. With his few remaining cents he bought candy for his son. Joyfully he made his way eastward along the elm-shaded highway. Soon the honking of car horns, the swirling dust, and the hubbub of the town were all gone without a trace, dissipated in the narrow rays of pure sunlight.

From his childhood, Hulk had always been attracted to the bustle of the town, to the candy glimpsed through store windows and the popsicles that came out of growling refrigerators. But the strange thing was that he only had to set foot on the road home (in those days it wasn't paved, and the trees hadn't been planted) for his heart to feel as free and relaxed as if it had been washed clean in springwater. The pure air that wafted in from the meadows was sweeter than any candy, more refreshing than any popsicle. Nature was the gentlest and fairest of mothers, sharing her bounty equally with all creatures.

Hulk adjusted the straps on his basket, took a deep breath, and called out behind him: "Come on, Lazybones!" The dog bounded up and made a friendly lunge at his leg. Hulk breathed deeply, utterly content, submerging himself in the warmth and heady scent of that lazy spring day like a bee immersing itself in the fragrance of a flower. His eyes crinkled with admiration as he gazed ahead of him. This is truly spring, he thought. This is what a park ought to look like. What's so great about that so-called park in town? Just a few fenced-in pear trees and a couple of roses with name tags! But here, as far as the eye could see, were rape-seed flowers of bright, stunning yellow, set off by glossy green leaves, stretching up toward white clouds floating in the deep blue of the sky. And their fragrance! It lay across the road solid as a wall, caught in his throat, and made his heart tremble. He felt like giving voice to a joyful anthem, but then a memory made him chew his thick lips in silence—in his long-ago school days, his singing had never made the grade.

Fortunately Lazybones was fully in harmony with his master's mood, and animals aren't expected to sing in tune. His barking was full of passion and inspiration. Butterflies flitted among the golden flowers, swallows dipped and rose behind the raised paths that bordered the fields. Dainty pink buds burst from the young elms by the roadside, and under the trees, where few passersby had trodden, grass grew lush and verdant. Flowers red as flame bloomed in undergrowth the deep blue-green of a lake, and out of the clumps of flowers rose graceful round heads of lantern grass, bobbing as they caught the breeze.

Lazybones kept up his barking, inspired by the beauty of the spring day. He frolicked around, jumping up now and then to lick at his master's clothes. "Get lost!" With feigned impatience, Hulk swung a foot at him: "Don't be a menace!" Lazybones was delighted with the attention. He knew his master had no intention of kicking him, so he persisted, digging his teeth into Hulk's pant leg and refusing to let go. Hulk pointed ahead: "Look, Lazybones, there's a bee. Catch it!"

At his master's command, the dog sprang forward—not for the bee, though. Instead he went chasing off after a bobbing yellow butterfly. With the slightest flutter of its wings, the butterfly eluded the flailing claws and flitted elegantly away. Furious, Lazybones leaped a second time, but the butterfly dodged again and flew off toward the field of golden rape with the dog in hot pursuit.

Hulk was mightily amused: "Hoho, I've heard of dogs that catch rats, but this is the first butterfly hound I've come across!" The next time he looked, Lazybones had bounded into the rape field and was swallowed up in the glimmering sea of golden flowers.

"Lazybones!" he called, but the only response was from a flock of golden orioles that flew straight up out of the sea of yellow toward the blue of the sky.

As Hulk surveyed the havoc that his dog was wreaking in the quiet and fragrant world beneath the rape flowers, his thick lips creased in a smile. Why shouldn't he feel joyful? The sunlight, the scent and color of the flowers, distilled into a fiery liquor that seared his soul, making his head dizzy and his feet weightless. Who said he was ill-fated? His luck was as good as anyone's!

For a start there was his wife, Aying. Hulk wasn't a man to brag, but there wasn't a woman within thirty miles with looks to touch hers, and even in town there couldn't have been many in her class. She was neither too tall nor too short, too plump nor too thin. She had a little red mouth and jet-black eyes, deep dimples, and thick eyelashes; her hair was utterly enchanting, with a natural wave and a thick fringe framing her forehead. People said she was as cute as a doll in a display case or a mannequin in a shopwindow. In the days when the Model Operas were in vogue, she was given the nickname Model Girl.

When the Model Girl was eighteen or nineteen, there were always matchmakers at her door, presenting the credentials of accountants, teachers, carpenters, and tailors . . . in fact every gainfully employed young man in the district put himself forward. But the Model Girl's mother was determined to marry her daughter to none other than the perfect son-in-law, and her criteria were extremely rigorous. She examined all the suitors' qualifications, but none of them met her demands. The girl had to remain closeted away in her "maiden's apartments," little imagining she'd still be waiting there at twenty-five or that she'd end up married to a great ass like Hulk.

There were those who were of the opinion that she had married beneath herself and that if Hulk had not come by this wife of his so undeservedly he would certainly have been a bachelor all his days. When he heard this kind of talk, Hulk would always pretend to get in a huff: "Huh, let's see if you can get yourself a wife the same 'undeserved' way I did!" In his heart of hearts he knew there was some truth in what people said; he really was hardly the proper match for this angelic Model Girl. It was a once-in-a-lifetime chance, but if fate is on your side, you can sometimes pick up gold nuggets beside the road. The penniless Hulk had found himself a wife, even if it was undeserved, and who else was there who had luck like that? He chuckled as he walked along, happiness enveloping him like the fragrance in the air. He turned round and yelled, "Lazybones!"

There was no response from the dog. The yellow flowers

of the rape gleamed in his eye, taking him back to another incomparably beautiful day eight years before.

It was spring then too, the same warmth and the same fragrance. He and Lazybones were out hunting and found themselves by just such a beautiful field two villages from home. For all the ground they'd covered, they hadn't caught so much as a feather. It was past noon, and Hulk's stomach was beginning to rumble.

Suddenly a badger came rushing out of the bamboo grove, right toward them! The beast couldn't have picked a better moment from Hulk's point of view—the adrenalin revived him more than a draft of ginseng could ever have done, and he and Lazybones charged into the bamboos in hot pursuit.

The badger was cunning—it shot back to its sett and vanished. But Hulk was no fool: he could match wits with this animal. Badgers try to trick the hunter by having a number of bolt-holes to their setts; if a badger escapes down one hole, it will invariably emerge a good distance away and scamper off. If you wait by the first hole and think you'll catch it there, you've fallen for the trick. So Hulk blocked this hole with a rock and ordered Lazybones to hunt out the other ones. Lazybones raced into a patch of rape to the east of the bamboo. Hulk yelled angrily, "Lazybones! Back here!" but the dog took no notice. Just as had happened today, plants were knocked flying, and birds flew up in alarm. It was as though a tornado had struck, and from its vortex came Lazybones' frantic barking. Lazybones was calling him—the dog must be on to something! Delighted, he swept the dense growth aside and hurried over. When the dog saw his master coming, he stopped barking and lay flat on the ground, growling. Hulk was satisfied that this was the bolt-hole, so he ordered, "In, boy!" He pointed to the hole, meaning that Lazybones should go in and flush the badger out.

But either the hole was too narrow, or the dog had some inkling of the viciousness of badgers; Lazybones just scampered around the hole whimpering agitatedly, not daring to go in. Hulk realized he was going to have to find another way to get the badger out of its hole. There were two options, smoke or soak. But for smoke you need matches, and to soak you need a bucket. He had neither, and he didn't know anyone in the village. What could he do? Hulk stamped his feet in frustration. It was at this moment that he saw a vision of loveliness: a girl in a red jacket, emerging from a cottage by the field. For a few seconds his head was reeling so much that he forgot the badger. She was so beautiful! Hulk had never seen anyone like her! He couldn't tell what it was about her that attracted him so much; he just felt that she was totally different from other village girls. Everything that lay before him—yellow flowers, green bamboos, emerald willows, verdant pines—it was all made more vivid because she was there.

Confusion struck him dumb. Then Lazybones' persistent barking brought him to his senses: "You're like Pigsy in Gao Village—nothing on your mind but sex! What's it to you if the young lady's so pretty? The ugly girls in your own village won't give you a second glance, so you needn't go losing your head over this one!" After a few moments, his dizzy spell passed. But he still wanted to talk to her—there was no harm in that, surely? Anyway, he had to have a bucket to soak this badger out! His mind made up, he strode over.

The girl was humming as she hung out her washing. Her movements were deft and as rhythmic as her tune. She was so engrossed in her work that she failed to notice the approaching Hulk, and this made him all the more nervous, standing awkwardly and wondering how to address her. If this stranger had been a man and younger, Hulk could have called him "Little Brother"; if older, then "Elder Brother." Older still, and "Uncle" would have been appropriate, or even "Grandpa." A mature woman could have been addressed as "Aunty," "Mama," or "Grandma" without fear of giving offense. Only younger girls like this one presented a problem. "Little Sister" would be too familiar, while "Elder Sister" would put him at an unnecessary disadvantage since he was clearly her senior. What was he to do?

Hulk scratched his head and pondered for a long time before coming up with a compromise. He went up to her and said solemnly, "Little Elder Sister!" Combining the "Little" with the "Elder Sister" seemed like a real stroke of genius on his part. The girl in the red jacket had in all likelihood never been addressed in this odd way before. She stared at him in astonishment. Nervously, Hulk stammered: "Little . . . er . . . Little Elder Sister!" Finally it dawned on the girl that "Little Elder Sister" was herself, and she burst into a fit of giggles. Hulk was taken aback, but now that he was started, he was determined to see the matter through. So he stumbled through the business about borrowing the bucket.

She smiled: "What do you need the bucket for?"

"I've caught a badger . . . well, no, I haven't actually, but I've found his hole." The thought of that splendid badger made him more animated, almost eloquent. The girl's curiosity was piqued, so as she hurried off to get the bucket, she said, "I've never seen a badger. Don't forget to show it to me when you catch it."

"Sure." Hulk grabbed the bucket and ran off. By this point he'd have caught a devil if it had been down the hole. He'd given his word to the girl, and this was a sacred vow that must be kept.

The badger was not disposed to be cooperative. It took Hulk and Lazybones until sunset to catch it, by which time both were covered in mud. A jubilant Hulk took the badger to show the girl.

"So that's what a badger looks like!" he girl stroked the thick fur. "See how fierce it is—even when it's dead, it still bares its fangs."

"That's right," Hulk agreed, very pleased with himself. "It's not too big, but just take a look at those teeth! Even the bravest of hunting dogs is afraid of a badger. It'll go for a dog's throat—one crunch, and the windpipe's gone."

"Really?" The girl sounded quite alarmed.

Hulk was more full of himself than ever. He boasted, "But this one was no match for me. As soon as he stuck his head out of the hole, I was there to give it a whack. He's nothing to be afraid of now he's dead."

"This badger's pretty valuable, eh?" She asked cautiously.

"Every part of the badger's body is worth something. See the pelt, how thick and glossy it is; that'll fetch quite a bit. Badger meat is very nutritious, better than a tonic for the weak and elderly. Then there's the oil—you rub that on frostbite, and you'll never have the problem again. . . ."

The words gushed out of Hulk's mouth. So intently was he talking that he didn't see she had wandered off. She had noticed that some of the rape plants in her family's plot had fallen over and had gone over to find out what was the matter. Then she saw the full story—a large number of plants had been knocked over, and a patch in the middle where the badger's sett had been was completely flattened. In her excitement over the badger, it hadn't occurred to her to ask where it had been caught. Now all was revealed. She stormed up to Hulk and pointed at him furiously: "Look what you've done! See how much of our crop you've ruined! You . . . you'll have to pay us back!"

Hulk recognized that he was at fault. But what was he to do? He had no money, and apart from his gun and dog, the only thing he had of any value was the badger. He scratched his head with a muddy hand. The in a burst of inspiration, he handed over the badger: "Here, this'll pay you back!"

The girl was taken by surprise. A few stalks of rape aren't worth that much, and she hadn't really expected any compensation; she had only spoken as she did because she was upset at the damage. Now as she saw him standing bashfully before her, the corners of her mouth twitched, and she started giggling again.

Hulk hadn't really intended to part with the badger. If he hadn't been in such a state, he'd have realized that the badger was worth way more than the rape. But the girl's laugh had a spellbinding power, making him unable to retract his offer, and the more she insisted she couldn't take it, the more he tried to force it on her. Back and forth it went, until their voices roused the people in the cottage. The door swung open, and a grizzled old man emerged. "Aying," he demanded, "what's all this row?"

Hulk figured out that this must be the girl's father, and his heart sank. But after the old man had asked him his business, he merely twiddled his whiskers, said, "Astounding!" and courteously invited him in to sit down for a while.

Hulk had no idea what the old fellow was thinking of. What he did know, however, was that nobody had ever treated him so politely before. A badger was, in the final analysis, nothing so precious that he couldn't give it to them, and besides, the girl had such a lovely smile. He strode confidently into the cottage.

The old man was indeed the girl's father, and the invalid lying on the bed was her mother. As they entered, the old man told his daughter to fetch a basin of hot water for their guest to wash in. Aying wasn't that keen, but to maintain her father's dignity she did as he asked. To Hulk, the basin that she gave him with her own fair hands held the sweetest dew the gods could bestow. He plunged his whole head into the water, and soon the mud and sweat of the day's hunting had been washed away. The old man examined Hulk's physiognomy meticulously: "A fine face! Broad forehead, fleshy nostrils, full mouth, big ears . . . have you eaten?"

This was likely a conventional politeness rather than the offer of a meal, but the literal minded Hulk shook his head no. The mention of food made him realize that he was terribly hungry. His straightforwardness seemed to be to the old man's liking, and he ordered his daughter to prepare a meal. Still trying to figure out what had got into her father, Aying hurried into the kitchen to fry up some leftover rice and make a bowl of egg-drop soup.

To Hulk, that simple meal of fried rice and soup was ambrosia and nectar. The old man made idle conversation as Hulk ate; then, judging his moment, he asked abruptly, "And how many are there in your esteemed family?" Caught by surprise, Hulk said the first thing that came into his head: "Er, there's just the two of us." He shoveled in another mouthful of rice and mumbled: "One of them's me. . . ."

"And the other?"

"The other? It's . . . er. . . ." He yelled at the doorway, "Lazybones! Here boy!"

The old man burst out laughing. Aying sniggered behind her hand. Hulk put down his bowl and chopsticks and rubbed his full stomach. I've eaten their food, he thought, and I've damaged their crops. It wouldn't be proper to leave without giving something in return. So as he was leaving he insisted he should leave the badger with them, and this time he really meant it. The old man shook his head and pushed it away, repeating polite clichés that Hulk couldn't understand the half of. It even got to the point where the sick woman heaved herself up and joined in: "Young man, those animals are hard to catch, and you've worked all day for it. How can we possibly take it away from you?" Only the girl said nothing, biting her lip to stop herself from laughing at this boneheaded stranger.

Hulk was dismayed at their refusal to take the badger. He pointed to the sick woman and said, "Well, then, think of it as something for Aunty here to help her get better."

Now the old man couldn't refuse it. "Indebted, profoundly indebted," he muttered and accepted the gift.

For days after this, Hulk felt relaxed and satisfied. It didn't seem that he had lost a badger, rather that he had gained something for nothing. This feeling was all the stronger when he closed his eyes and remembered the way the girl had talked to him, her smile, his indescribable joy as she brought him the basin of water. At these times he would wish he could have stayed a little longer in the family's cottage. But at other times this sense of well-being would desert him, leaving him lonely and frustrated. Then he would chastise himself: "However nice she is, she's not yours, so what the hell are you doing thinking about her?" After this he would calm down a little. It was impossible not to think of her at all, so he did his best to think about her less often but more thoroughly, savoring every detail as a child lingers over a candy, trying to keep the sweetness on his tongue a moment longer.

Then, out of the blue, Hulk's wildest dreams came true! One evening after work, when he had stretched out on the bed and was preparing to savor that ineradicable sweetness once more, the old man came in. "I'll marry my daughter to you if you'll take her," he said.

Hulk sat bolt upright on his bed and stared in disbelief at the old man. There he stood, fiddling with his whiskers and wagging his head. "The girl's name is Aying," he added. "You've met her. . . ."

What miracles life can hold! From that moment, Hulk had tumbled into a world of delight, his life as joyful as dancing in the clouds. Now his son was seven years old and as attractive as his mother. Hulk beamed hugely and rubbed his flapping ears, which the sun had scorched bright red. From childhood he had been told that flap ears were lucky, and maybe his present good fortune was indeed thanks to these vast ears of his.

The sun was at its height as Hulk and Lazybones returned to the village. Crab-apple blossoms by the roadside shone red in the sunshine. Clothing and lengths of cloth of every conceivable fabric and color hung on the balconies, looking like the flags of all nations. Hulk took pleasure from them all. If I make money on these rabbits, he thought, then I'll buy Aying a wool coat in dark green. Nowadays girls get a smart new coat for their weddings, but poor Aying had married him without even a decent jacket to her name. And then, of course, she would have to have wool to knit a couple of sweaters, one saffron like that one hanging over the balcony at the south end of the village, and one blue like he'd seen at the store in town. Aying was still young, barely thirty. He should get her to dress up a little. . . .

"Sister, those pants of yours are really neat. They're such a great color, and the creases are so sharp!"

"Of course, they're pure Dacron; they won't crinkle however you fold them. You should get a pair yourself."

Women's voices wafted toward him on the warm breeze. Hulk looked back and saw two young women companionably hanging pairs of pants on their balcony. His heart started to pound, and his pace slowed to a crawl.

—4—

While Hulk was carrying his rabbits home and relishing the warm spring sun, his wife, Aying, was hanging clothes out to air. In fact, every family in the village was doing the same thing. Every spring, just before the period of downpours known as the plum rains, peasant women pick a warm and breezy day to air all their clothes in the sun, to stop them from going mouldy. This is called the "spring airing."

The spring airing gives everyone a chance to show off and compare their possessions. Housewives bring out the clothes that they keep in trunks because they are too good to wear. There are woolens and tweeds, silks and satins, and in recent years synthetics like Acrilan, Dacron, and nylon as well. The well-to-do naturally take the opportunity to flaunt their wealth, while poorer families respond as best they can by hanging out a length of homespun or a bundle of cotton padding. Although there is no set date for the spring airing, everyone always does it on the same day. All it takes is just one family to start hanging things out, and everyone else joins in.

Noon is the high point of the day, the time for women to go visiting and make comparisons. Young girls ogle admiringly, while their seniors do their best to hide their envy, and, in the time it takes to eat a meal, judgment will have been passed: Mrs. So-and-So has so much homespun, over eighty seven-meter lengths of it! Mrs. So-and-So has more woolen jackets than anyone else, more than twenty! Mrs. So-and-So has the most knitting wool. Mrs. So-and-So's family has a new woolen carpet. . . . And so on.

At times like these, women like to show off their fashion sense. So while everyone is clucking admiringly over a piece of clothing, there will be someone who cuts in before the others have a chance to speak, "That cloth's called Melton; my husband bought some like it last year in Shanghai." Or else, with studied unconcern, "I've got a pair of flannel pants just like those!"

Most of the really good clothes that are hung out to air the women got at the time of their marriages. A girl from a respectable family is supposed to go to her new home with clothes enough to last her half a lifetime, though there's no knowing how many of these fineries ever actually come anywhere near their owners' bodies. The only chance to create an impression with them comes in this one noon hour every spring.

Aying felt dowdy by comparison with the others. Her mother had died the year she married Hulk, and the family was deeply in debt. Hulk wasn't the kind to set money aside, so there hadn't been any pretty clothes for their wedding. Now that all the villagers were airing their clothes she had to do the same, but she didn't join the procession from house to house. She laid out a couple of bamboo blinds by the door and spread out on them what little she possessed—some old lengths of cloth, a camel-hair jacket, an Acrilan coat, and the heavy tracksuit that Hulk wore in winter. She moved slowly and deliberately, as if to indicate to the watching world that her trunk wasn't empty but held more for her to unpack.

In fact there was one more thing right at the bottom of the trunk—a pair of permanent-press woolen pants. These pants were her pride and joy—and the only token of affection that Hulk had ever given her. Had it not been for that pair of pants, she might even have refused the marriage.

There had been no shortage of suitors for the young Aying. If only her mother hadn't been so hard to please, she would never have had the bad luck to meet Hulk outside their cottage. After her mother became ill, however, the family's circumstances declined sharply, and the stream of matchmakers slowed to a trickle. The one man who was prepared to put up a sizable amount of money as a betrothal gift was unceremoniously shown the door by Aying's father. "My daughter is not for sale," he announced haughtily.

But he really took to Hulk. Aying never suspected what was in her father's mind and was appalled when he raised the possibility: "Ugh! The thought of it! Do you think I could go out with a clod like that?"

The old man snorted disapprovingly. He was against this new fad for despising rustic ways and admiring Western affectations. As he explained to his daughter, there were some men who had bad luck written all over their faces; it was simply absurd for such people to dress themselves up and try to talk their way to the top with their oily mouths and greasy tongues. "I don't care how rich those guys are," he insisted. "I've no time for any of them!"

When his daughter remained silent, the old man tried another tack: "Sweetheart, what good is a man if all he has is money? Only honesty and loyalty last a lifetime. I've seen more of the world than you have, and I'm not easily fooled. As soon as I met Hulk I knew he was a man of honor. His face is lucky—just look at the size of those ears! He has fortune on his side, and he'll do all right in the end."

This line of reasoning must have seemed pretty bizarre to a girl in her mid-twenties. But since this was her father speaking, Aying couldn't express herself too strongly. She pouted: "We can't live on his ears, however big they are! How can I face anyone if I marry him?"

The old man shook his head and sighed: "There's more to consider than money. Precious metals can be used up; you'd do better with honesty and loyalty as your capital!"

His words struck some chord in Aying's heart. What village girl doesn't want a husband she can depend on all her life? But when she remembered Hulk's swarthy face and stupid expression, she still wasn't keen: "He's probably never been near a girl in his life. What can he know about romance?"

"Silly girl, it's only a man like that who can truly love you! Men who spend all their time chasing women aren't worth having!" The old man chuckled.

Aying blushed and pursed her lips prettily: "Good-mannered young men always take their girls to Shanghai for a day out, don't they? He should at least take me for a stroll in the county town."

Sensing that her resistance was weakening, her father chuckled again: "Okay, then, Hulk can take you to Shanghai tomorrow and buy you whatever you fancy!"

Aying didn't take her father's words too seriously, but to her surprise Hulk did indeed show up bright and early the next morning. He'd left his gun and dog at home, his clothes were new, and he'd brought two bottles of rice spirit and some pastries. The old man could hardly contain himself, babbling delightedly as Aying ushered his intended son-in-law into the cottage. Aying sneaked a glance at him as well. It's true what they say—a lick of paint can do wonders for a Buddha, and clothes can make the man. Though Hulk was only wearing a plain factory-made suit, he looked a different man from the one she'd seen the last time. He'd had a haircut and a shave, and now she noticed his broad forehead, his strong chin, and the twinkle in his eyes. His complexion was dark, to be sure, but the high nose stood well on his large face, and he looked gentle, even handsome, if a little rough-hewn. No wonder her father had said Hulk's physiognomy was well favored. Aying blushed and bowed her head to cover the embarrassment.

The old man's beady eyes were sizing Hulk up as well. He slapped him on the back: "Not bad!" He grinned: "These days the girls in Shanghai all want a tall man. They'll all be after you when they see how big you are!"

Hulk gave a forced laugh and interrupted: "I've come to take Aying out for a day in Shanghai." Now that his prepared statement had been delivered, the sweat began to pour off his head, either in reaction to what the old man had said, or because he had got hot on the way over. The old man saw how nervous Hulk was and said, "Off to Shanghai, are you? Grand idea. Youngsters like you should be out having a good time on a lovely day like this. It's early yet, no need to hurry. Sit down, and rest awhile, loosen your clothes, have some tea. Look how warm you are."

While he was waiting for Aying to come in with the tea, Hulk took off his jacket, revealing the old undershirt he wore underneath. The undershirt was short for him and full of holes. By the time he realized that this might make a poor impression, it was too late—Aying had seen. But actually he hadn't made a bad impression. Quite the opposite—she had seen the powerful physique that the worn undershirt couldn't cover, and his bulging muscles aroused something in her that she didn't fully understand.

With no further prompting from the old man, the beautiful Aying and her young man, Hulk, caught the bus for Shanghai. The emerald fields slipped by, to be replaced by tall buildings and crowded streets. The world about them was suddenly transformed.

The normally vivacious Aying became very quiet in this unfamiliar territory, away from the bamboo groves and little bridges that she saw every day. In among the densely packed buildings and the endless stream of pedestrians, she lost her sense of direction. Her only previous trip to Shanghai had been a primary school visit to the Western Suburbs Park. Hulk was different, though. He was the kind of man who will chat to anyone, so though he'd been in Shanghai only once before, to transport fertilizer, he knew where to go to find the bustling streets and the high-quality goods. With barely a sideways glance at the smaller shops and narrow alleys, he led Aying straight to Nanking Road.

Hulk stopped in front of the imposing doors of a department store. After studying the sign, he beamed at Aying: "This is the best clothing store in Shanghai. Let's go in and take a look!" Then he swept the doors open and strode in with the air of a man of unlimited resources who fully intends to buy everything in the store.

Hulk was inspired. He marched up to the counter and demanded, "Please show us some women's trousers, the best you have!"

The salesmen was sufficiently experienced to recognize that this was a customer out of the ordinary. "Our best . . . certainly," he murmured, wondering how best to deal with the request. They had dozens of different kinds of trousers in the store, all of them superior in their own way. He understood that this was a fellow in from the countryside who wanted to impress the young lady, so he favored them with his best sales patter: "Comrade, is it your wish to purchase winter-weight pants like these, or would you prefer summer pants, or perhaps something for spring and fall? We have winter weight in twill, flannel, or Melton. For summer wear, the better natural fabrics are Versailles and Palace, or else you could go with a synthetic. There's a good selection for spring and fall as well: wool-Dacron blends, pure Dacron, gabardine . . . what have you in mind?"

This earnest and comprehensive introduction to the store's products had Hulk frowning with consternation. He always wore the same pair of old cotton pants from the coldest frosts of winter to the hottest spell in summer, and they suited him just fine. Never would he have guessed that city folk had so many choices—a pair for spring, another for summer! These people must be so busy changing their pants they have no time for anything else!

But the wad of banknotes in his pocket made him press on. A gleam appeared on his oily face: "Never mind about the Nywool or the Dacrilon," he said. "Just tell me this—which pair is most expensive?"

In answer, the salesman smiled, glanced at Aying, and selected a pair of pure wool pants in olive green, which he placed on the counter.

Aying was delighted. She loved the color, the material, and the style. When she tried them on, the fit was perfect—they could have been made to measure. They were elegant yet understated, crisply pressed yet soft. She turned around a few times in front of the mirror, admiring the pants. Hulk had been planning to ask if they had anything even more expensive, but when he saw how delighted she was, he just grinned and paid up.

That trip to Shanghai won Aying's heart. She liked Hulk for his generosity and even more for his manliness and authority. One month later she was married in her "most expensive" pants.

These "most expensive" pants greatly enhanced her social standing. She had a good figure, and when she showed it off in her marvelous pants, she looked better than anyone else, no matter how drab her jacket was. Other village women might be better off and have more clothes than she did, but none had pants to compare with hers! Even the old lady next door would stroke them admiringly and murmur, "Such lovely material, so thick but so fine. I'd never have thought that great lout Hulk would have such an eye for quality!"

Her daughter-in-law objected: "You get what you pay for, Ma. Give me fifty yuan, and I'll go straight to Shanghai and get a pair like that for myself."

This kind of talk was music to Aying's ears. Later, however, the daughter-in-law borrowed the pants to wear to a wedding and kept them for three days. When she returned them, there was a grease stain on the right leg. Aying was upset for days, but she didn't feel she could make a scene. All she could do was scrub the spot with a toothbrush dipped in soap. She got the stain out, but the spot stood out from the area around it, slightly lighter in color and more susceptible to mold. So every year at this time she would take the pants out, inspect them, brush them, and air them out so they wouldn't go moldy—this was the last and the most important item on her agenda for the spring airing.

Just as she was about to continue, there was a burst of laughter, and a group of visiting women swept in like a cheerful whirlwind.

"What new clothes have you got, Aying?"

"You don't have any nice stuff out yet. You must be hiding it from us."

Aying smiled wryly: "I don't have any new clothes—if I did, I'd have hung them out, wouldn't I?"

"Then you should go out and buy yourself a new Dacron jacket," one of the girls advised her earnestly. "You've got such a nice figure, I'm sure something gathered in at the waist would look lovely on you. It's not like Acrilan, which looks good when it's new but goes crinkly later."

"Stupid brat!" Someone gave the girl a slap on the shoulder. "Do you think your Aunty Aying can't get dressed up? You should see her in her green pants; they're quite something. . . ."

Aying was delighted to hear this. She smoothed out a few stray hairs and murmured modestly, "I still think pure wool is the best. Synthetics all lose their value sooner or later. Only wool keeps its price."

The girls were quite impressed and all the more anxious to see the pants. As the chorus of giggling continued, Aying went inside to fetch them. But the pants were gone!

She clearly remembered putting them in the red trunk on top of the closet, but when she took all the things out of the trunk, there was no sign of them. The women at the door became impatient and crowded in. Poor Aying was so upset she had to bite her lip to stop herself from crying.

No other household in this simple and law-abiding community had had clothing go missing. Everyone thought Aying must have forgotten where she had put the pants, so they joined in the search. As they rummaged through her boxes, Aying blushed for shame at the rags and tatters they uncovered. They even came on some dried ground beetles from years before, but the pants were still missing.

The women gave up and went away, leaving Aying alone and desolate in the chaos of her room. At that moment Hulk returned. Aying charged over and demanded, "Have you seen my green pants?" Hulk blanched; he went straight into the kitchen without a word, put down his basket, and squatted down to take out the baby rabbits.

"Where'd you get those rabbits?" Aying asked suspiciously. Hulk had asked for money a few days before, but she had refused to give him any.

"Did you borrow the money, or what?" she continued. Still no answer. She started to get angry: "Don't act dumb! If we lose money again, don't think you'll get a cent out of me!"

Hulk looked up at her nervously and mumbled, "Got a headache." Then he stood up, shambled into the bedroom, and collapsed on the bed. She didn't want to pursue the matter with him in this state, so she contented herself with yelling, "If you've got to lie down, at least take your clothes off—don't get all that mess on the bed!" Listlessly, Hulk pulled off his clothes and tossed them aside, then pulled the quilt over his head and went to sleep.

Angrily Aying picked up his clothes, and, as she began to fold them, a scrap of paper dropped out of one of the pockets. It was a receipt from a pawnshop—that bastard Hulk had pawned her pants! And one glance at the basket of rabbits told her why! Her nose tingled; then the tears poured down her face. Her life was utterly wretched! The day she married him, she had begun to realize that the qualities she had seen as virtues were really faults. He was utterly irresponsible about finances, raising chickens one day and beetles the next, forever chopping and changing. If he wasn't getting himself criticized so he had to cut off his dog's tail, then he was losing money. Everyone else was living in two-story houses, and here they were in a two-room hovel! She had taken over the family finances a couple of years ago, and things had begun to look up a bit; they had even managed to save a couple of hundred yuan. But at what cost! She hadn't bought a single article of clothing for herself, and when she saw her son salivating as the other kids ate ice cream, she had to agonize over whether she could afford four miserable cents for a popsicle! How could she have known that Hulk would think so little of all her sacrifices that when she refused him money for rabbits he would steal her pants and pawn them! If this got out, such reputation as she had would be in tatters!

Aying felt hurt and angry. Seeing her husband curled up

like a great shrimp under the quilt, she grabbed hold of their carrying pole and walloped Hulk with it, as she had his bobtail dog so many years before.

—5—

Hulk cowered under the quilt and readied himself for the next blow. But none came. He pushed the quilt down slightly and peered out. The room was empty. He remembered that he had seen his son Amao catching earthworms by the wall as he came in, so he called out, "Amao, Amao!"

When there was no answer, he began to feel anxious. He rolled back the quilt and sat up. The black patent-leather purse his wife always carried was gone, and so were her washcloth and toothbrush.

"This is awful!" he moaned. If only there had been a medicine for remorse, he would have bought it whatever the cost.

His good luck might have got him one wife "undeservedly," but how could he expect it to work for him a second time? Aying was pretty, capable, gentle, and clever . . . and if she had clouted him with the carrying pole just now, well, he'd deserved it! She'd have been well within her rights if she'd hit him a few more times! Why did he have to be such a bastard, he cursed himself. Was there another man in the world who was such a bastard? Sure the rabbits were cute, and it would have upset him not to buy them, but a guy shouldn't pawn his wife's best pants, should he? Hulk did not see how he could have acted as he did. He had lost his head—he must have been possessed by an evil spirit. Then he started thinking about how good Aying's family had been to him. He had lost both of his parents when he was still in his teens, and from that time until his marriage there had been nobody to care for him. As he hadn't a cent to his name, his father-in-law had let him have Aying without a bride-price. Not only that—the old man had even given him a hundred yuan! That day, Aying's father had hurried over to Hulk's place and made all the arrangements for the marriage. Then, as he left, he had slipped Hulk the cash and whispered that he should take Aying to Shanghai the next day and show her a good time so that she would like him. That was why he had been so bold about taking her to town and buying her the pants. Poor Aying had never known that the money that bought her pants had been her father's. She had always thought so much of those pants and thought it had been her husband who had provided the money to buy them. I'm inhuman, thought Hulk, I'm a brute, I'm a filthy object that even pigs and dogs would turn up their noses at, I'm. . . .

That was as far as he got. His nose tingled, his throat tightened, and his chest felt constricted. He wanted to weep, to bawl, to box his own ears; but just at that moment, the door pushed open, and light feet pattered up to him. Then something warm and furry flopped onto the bed and nestled in beside him. It was Lazybones!

The dog's warm tongue licked the back of Hulk's hand, and a cold nose rubbed against his arm. Lazybones' warmth seemed to flow into his master's breast; Hulk's heart trembled, and the tears flowed down.

He thought back to his wedding night. He had barred the front door and taken his new bride in his arms when the bedroom door had been pushed open in just the same gentle way, feet had padded across the floor, and Lazybones had snuggled up against him. Hulk had always shared his bed with Lazybones, but on that sweetest of nights, the dog's action caught him unawares. He hugged the dog and told his bride to stroke him too. Aying recoiled in disgust, so Hulk had to push the dog onto the floor. Poor Lazybones watched resentfully as the couple enjoyed their first night of wedded bliss.

It all seemed like yesterday. Now his wife had gone, taking their son. Was he left with only Lazybones to help him through the long dark nights?

Hulk's customary resilience was shaken. He shivered as a new thought came to him: "It's so hard to be a man," he groaned. Aside from his limited academic attainments, he had always felt he was as good as anyone at anything. Whether he was climbing trees to steal eggs or diving in the river for fish, it had been his blessing since childhood to be bigger and stronger than others. Whatever fate had dealt him, he had endured, insisting that "everyone has his own piece of heaven," his muscular body pulsating with controlled power. And since it's human nature for even the most abject beggar to wish that rice will fall from the sky, how could a strong fellow like Hulk be satisfied with his poverty? How could he rest content when his wife had no new clothes to wear and he could never afford a treat for his son? Of course he couldn't. He wanted to turn things around. He wanted a big house with a balcony like other villagers had, and he wanted a television so that he wouldn't have to trudge a mile to watch the one at brigade headquarters. He wasn't feudal minded: he wanted his wife to perm her hair like a city girl and have different pants for every season the way city folk did. He wanted to be rich. So his reason for getting the rabbits wasn't only that he adored furry little animals; there was also the tantalizing prospect of wealth that the team leader had raised. What if the rabbits all flourished? What if he made a pile of money on them? Of course there was a certain risk involved, though it wasn't the prospect of losing money that bothered him as much as the contract he had signed with his father-in-law. . . .

"Daddy! Daddy!" Hulk's confused thoughts were interrupted by a clear young voice. Seven-year-old Amao stood before him, red-faced and panting. "Daddy, Grandpa wants to see you," said the boy, his innocent young face somehow like both his parents.

"What . . . what's Grandpa doing? Did he say Dad was no good?"

"No." The boy shook his head.

Hulk felt relieved: "What did he say?"

Amao looked around him: "He asked me who did wrong, and I told him it was Mummy 'cause she hit Daddy with the carrying pole and Daddy didn't do anything."

"That's my boy!" Hulk hugged Amao and kissed his cheek. "What else did Grandpa say?"

Amao frowned: "Grandpa said something about the last time. . . ."

The boy couldn't remember the rest of it, but Hulk knew perfectly well what that meant. It looked as if the old man were going to hold him to his solemn oath and enforce the contract they had drawn up. What was Hulk to do? The old man had been so good to him. If there were a divorce, he'd never be able to find such a good father-in-law again, to say nothing of a wife.

Amao touched Hulk's leg: "Daddy, does it hurt?"

Hulk shook his head: "No, not at all." It was true—the pain was in his heart, but he couldn't explain that to the child.

"I told Grandpa that Mummy injured your leg, Dad," Amao giggled. "You should pretend it hurts. Grandpa said if your leg was really hurt, it wouldn't be right to . . . um . . . divorce."

Hulk kissed his son's head ecstatically. Only my father-in-law can save me now, he thought, and with his help I'll get out of this one yet. But then another thought struck him: the contract was crystal clear—any more speculating, and it's divorce, and no use whining about it. His leg really wasn't hurt at all, and it wouldn't be right to pretend it was. He could only follow the decree of fate. After all, everyone has his own patch of heaven. . . .

With this in mind, he gritted his teeth, heaved his legs out of the bed, and grabbed hold of his son: "Let's go!"

Outside, the sun was shining. In its warmth, his whole body relaxed. Plants were in full bloom, and the chinaberry tree was putting out fresh green shoots. As Hulk surveyed the scene, his anxiety of a moment ago gradually dissipated. Since everything that happens in life is ordained, what's the point in getting upset? Life is unpredictable. He remembered that as a child he would always be thinking about food when he was supposed to be studying, so that in the end his parents had pulled him out of school to be a cowherd. How his classmates had jeered behind his back! This was all the more so when the local genius had passed the university entrance exams and the whole village had turned out to see him off to college. Someone mocked Hulk: "Just look at you. You've got fame and fortune written all over your face, and it's done you no good. Look how well he's done!" Hulk didn't get angry, just creased his thick lips in a smile and went off to look after his birds, fish, cats, and dog. And how did it all turn out? Three years later, the "college boy" was sent home for labor reform; his reputation was shot, and all the village kids could spit at him. And there was Hulk, an outstanding poor peasant representative in the Cultural Revolution! Even though Hulk was barely literate, the college boy had to sit obediently and listen to every word he said. Sure Hulk had had his own comeuppance in the "capitalist tails" movement, but what official was there who hadn't been fired at least once? That was no big deal; look at the guy who had been chairman of the poor peasant representatives, head of the county propaganda department, in charge of farming for the county and on track for a meteoric rise—he was lucky to stay out of the slammer when the Gang of Four was arrested, and he was still under observation. Hulk might be poor, but he was still in a far better position than those who were under house arrest or being investigated.

Thus consoled, Hulk's stride became firmer. Amao couldn't keep pace, so Hulk hoisted the boy up on his shoulders. What with the sun and the little boy on his back, Hulk was soon drenched in sweat. Even loosening his shirt didn't cool him down. "This hot so soon after the Festival of Graves," he grumbled. He squinted up at the sun as it blazed down from a clear blue sky and was struck by a sudden thought: the sun may be an oppressor today, but sooner or later it's going to be eaten by the dog in heaven!

Right—that had happened one year, though he had been too young to remember exactly when, but it was spring then, too, and as hot as today. He had been sitting in the kitchen eating a bowl of rice porridge. Suddenly the sky had gone dark, as if a thick gray fog were covering the earth, blacking out the green of the meadows outside the window. Then came a cacophony of drums, gongs, and firecrackers. When he ran out to take a look, he saw people banging away on washbasins and pans. They were yelling: "The dog in heaven is eating the sun! He's eating the sun!" He gazed up at the sky; a great chunk was bitten out of the scorching sun, and the remaining part was getting gradually smaller, as if it were being consumed by some unseen monster. He looked down at his porridge—it was so thin that he could see his reflection on its watery surface. What has this to do with me? he asked himself. If the sun gets eaten, it gets eaten. I might as well finish my porridge. Then another thought struck him: How could he sit bare chested on the woodpile and pick lice out of his clothes if not for the warmth of the sun? He benefited from the sun as much as anyone. So, instead of eating his gruel, he battered on the rim of the bowl with his chopsticks. The noise pleased him, so he kept it up for quite a while.

Of course, the sun is the sun, and after the dog in heaven swallows it, he always finds it too hot to digest and spits it out. On this occasion, if the village elders were to be believed, the dog crapped rather than spat it out because the sun's light was grayish for the next few days, with less than its usual potency, proving that it had been longer inside the dog's belly. But, crapped or spat, the sun was the sun, and today it was good and hot (a fact that Hulk credited, in part at least, to his own bowl banging). And Hulk was still Hulk, strong and brawny, his vitality undiminished. . . .

Maybe it wasn't so hard to be a man after all. Fate always seems to find you a way out of difficulties, just as boats always make it under bridges sooner or later. So deeply immersed in his thoughts was Hulk that when he finally looked up he was surprised to see that they had almost reached the familiar two-room cottage among the bamboos. He squatted to let his son down, then gently pushed the boy forward. "Go on," he said. "Find out what Grandpa's saying."

—6—

As Hulk stood nervously eavesdropping outside the window, Aying finished her catalog of his sins. Finally she sighed and said despairingly, "I've seen through him—he's like a coffin with the bottom fallen out—there's just no way it can be fixed. I can't live with him any more, so I'll just have to divorce him."

This last sentence rooted Hulk to the spot, motionless as a statue.

"Aying!" The old man shook his head, eased himself into the only chair in the room, and peered at her through half-closed eyes. He spoke slowly: "You have to put up with things in this life. The ancients had it that 'a man may be poor, but willpower can never be exhausted.' Even in poverty you can find contentment—that's a lesson you can learn from Hulk. What can you gain moping and complaining all day? Wu Zixu worried all night until his hair went white, and what good did it do him? Cheer up, and you might get rich someday. Everyone knows how Hongwu of the Ming suffered in his youth, and he ended up becoming an emperor! When he had nothing to eat, he took a job looking after a buffalo, and when his hunger was more than he could bear, he killed the buffalo and roasted it. Then, realizing he couldn't confess to what he had done, he cut off the animal's tail and stuffed it down a burrow. Then he told his uncle that the buffalo had bolted down the burrow and couldn't get out. The uncle didn't believe him, of course, but when he went over and pulled at the tail, a buffalo really did start bellowing. You see, he was just lucky. Now the Chongzhen Emperor, the last ruler of the same Ming dynasty, he had no luck at all, so he finished up hanging himself on Prospect Hill. The splendid landlord's residence at Zhu Village was razed at night by Song Jiang's entourage; in the Shang dynasty, Bi Gan was uncle to the tyrant Zhou and became prime minister. He was master of thousands, and servant of one, but still ended up with his heart cut out. . . ."

The more the old man talked, the more pleased with himself he became. As the words gushed forth, his potato-shaped head with its few remaining strands of hair made circles in the air. This was an indication that he was settling in for a major monologue. Aying interrupted peevishly: "Dad, what are you on about this time? I'm not interested, and I don't want to listen."

"What's that?" He opened his eyes wide, like a man waking from a dream, and stared in disbelief. What did you expect? he seemed to be asking. Do you think I'm going to allow you to divorce? No chance!

But his speech and its implications had no effect on Aying, who had been inured to his orations since infancy. She bit her lip angrily and blurted: "Dad! Just think, all my life I've only ever had that one decent pair of pants that I got married in, and that bottomless coffin sold them. How can I ever have any dignity again? I hate him, and I hit him with the carrying pole!"

"What's come over you?" The old man's head stopped revolving, and he sat bolt upright. "Where's your self-control? Last time it was the dog you hit, and you broke its leg; this time it's a person. How could you do such a thing? Which is more important, pants or people? If you've damaged his head, he might become an imbecile, and how will you live then?"

"I hit him on the back," she said softly.

"So, his back. You shouldn't have hit him there, you know.

He's got an injury." The old man wasn't to be mollified. Aying could see that this conversation wasn't going her way; she stamped her foot in frustration and reminded him: "Oh Dad, I only hit him through the quilt."

"You wouldn't give him a real beating," her father said, smiling to himself before moving back onto the offensive. "Have you forgotten how he hurt his back when he went out at night to catch a bird to make soup for you? That's how his back problem started. What's to be done if it flares up again because you hit him with a carrying pole? Could you face yourself?"

Aying bowed her head and was silent. Memories, like a fine rain, dampened the flames of her fury.

Amao's birth had been a difficult one. The placenta had not come out whole; Aying had lost so much blood she almost died, and they'd had no money for the transfusion she needed. Fortunately Hulk was type O and was able to donate his blood to her. As his blood flowed into her body, she was like a withered leaf taking in moisture and coming back to life. When she came to, she heard the girls who had come to visit her chattering excitedly: "Hulk's quarreling with the doctor." She jerked up in alarm, afraid that the idiot was making a scene. Later she found out that the doctor had already taken 300 cc's of blood, but Hulk was demanding that they take more. The doctor told him that they wouldn't take any more for fear of causing a shock to his system, but Hulk patted his chest and told them he was in fine shape and they could have a bucketful of the stuff if they wanted. Taking that little glass tube of it was an insult. The doctor put on his sternest expression and told Hulk it didn't matter how strong he was, they weren't taking any more. Hulk saw them trying to ignore him, so he stuck his arm through the window into the doctors' office and refused to take it out. The doctors were all in a hurry to get off work, and since there wasn't anything to be gained by trying to reason with him, they gave in and took another 200 cc's.

After they'd drawn the blood, they told him to rest, but he absolutely refused to heed their advice. He saw how all the other women in maternity had chicken soup to build them up, and as he didn't have a chicken at home, he was determined to go out and catch a game bird. He didn't dare do it by day, for fear of being arrested as a poacher, so he set out at night. It was dark and wet, and even with the faithful Lazybones to lead the way, he still felt a little nervous. What's more, he was weakened by giving so much blood. He slipped and fell back against a boulder. It was hours before he could get up.

When he staggered back into the hospital, he was barely recognizable. He was covered in mud, his back was twisted, his neck cricked, his hair soaked and plastered to his head, and his swarthy face pallid. His bobtail dog snuffled and sneezed as it hobbled along behind.

Everyone in the ward was horrified and at a loss to understand what had happened. Aying sat forward fearfully: "What did you . . . what's wrong with you?"

In answer, he proudly displayed the gamecock he had caught, saying happily, "I've heard that wildfowl are even more nourishing than domestic hens."

Aying gazed at him devotedly, unable to say a word.

"There's a gas ring in there. I'll borrow a pan and stew it for you."

"No! No!" she cried, seizing hold of his jacket.

"What is it? Do you feel ill? Should I call the doctor?" Hulk's face contorted as a spasm of pain shot through his back. Then he looked lovingly down at Aying and reached out a huge hand to tuck her in. When he saw that the hand was covered in mud, he hastily withdrew it. Even this slight movement strained his injured back, and he winced involuntarily.

"Your back!" wailed Aying. "Look how much it hurts you!"

"It's nothing, honestly!" Hulk forced a smile. "You rest and I'll make you some soup." With that he hobbled out. Aying was still very upset. She reached for the tin beside her and called after him, "At least have a piece of cake first—you must be starving!" But Hulk disappeared through the door without a backward glance.

Once he was out of the room, the maternity ward buzzed with excitement. All along the row of beds, the women tossed and sighed, eager to speak but finding it hard to express their feelings. First to break the silence was a fat woman in the bed opposite. "You're a lucky one!" she said, eyeing Aying with undisguised envy.

The woman in the next bed let out a long sigh of what sounded like agreement. Though it was obvious from her fair complexion and glasses that she was a woman of status, the scene that had just been played out had clearly moved her deeply. "I'm from the city," she said emotionally, "but living there isn't easy. You can rely on country people more. I'd be content to live as a peasant all my life if I could only find a man like that."

That tribute loosened everyone's tongue. The quiet peasant girl in the bed by the fat woman chipped in, "That's right, you need a good man to help you get by in this life. A pile of gold and silver isn't worth a husband's love."

"If I were Aying, I could die content right now!" added the quick-tongued fat woman.

Aying should have responded to all this praise, but her eyes were filled with tears, and her mouth was trembling so much she couldn't say a word. She'd never thought of Hulk as being much of a husband and had often wished she had married someone better placed; but a husband of higher status might have been less prepared to spare his blood, and that could have been the end of her. . . .

She was dabbing at her tears with a handkerchief when she saw Lazybones by her bed, shaking off the rain and giving her his most endearing look. She felt a surge of affection. Silently she opened the cookie tin, took out a piece of cake, and slipped it into his mouth. It was the first morsel of food she had ever given her husband's beloved dog.

Hulk returned shortly with the steaming broth. She watched him through her tears, at a loss for words. She never slept a wink that night, just hugged her quilt and wept. Hulk hunched over her bed and dozed; from time to time she would rub his shoulder, or else cradle his head tenderly on her breast, asking if his back hurt. When the doctor came on his morning rounds, Aying pointed to Hulk. "I'm fine," she said. "It's my husband you should be looking at. He's dislocated his back."

The doctor looked down in amazement at the rough giant of a man, then raised his hands in a gesture of helplessness: "I'm sorry, I'm an obstetrician." But the women in the ward all pleaded Hulk's case and recounted the story of how Hulk had caught the gamecock. The doctor was impressed. "Come with me," he said, and led his unusual obstetrical case out of the ward.

The sight of Hulk's twisted back as he followed the doctor out of the ward reduced Aying to tears again. Later, the passage of time and the vexations of married life clouded the image of that moment; but now that her father mentioned it, the vision came back to her as clear as the first time, plucking at her heartstrings, warming her spirit with inexpressible tenderness. . . .

Hulk remained outside the window. He heard all his father-in-law said, and then there was a long silence. He wasn't sure what the silence meant, and his heart raced. Lazybones scratched frantically at the base of the wall, and Hulk shushed him. Amao looked at him as if he were about to say something, but Hulk covered the boy's mouth. In a while, the sound of muffled sobbing wafted through the window. Anxiously he wondered whether tears meant good or bad news for him; then he remembered that on the day seven years earlier when he'd hurt his back, he'd heard the same crying sound coming from Aying's quilt. Hulk felt a rush of joy. Then the old man started again: "Aying, when you're unhappy, you ought to think of the good times; when you quarrel, you should think of your husband's merits. That way the two of you will live in harmony together, and you won't lose your temper so often. Think of the year Amao was born—you might not have pulled through if it hadn't been for Hulk. I still think I was right to take a shine to the fellow. Of course, on this occasion he acted irresponsibly, and . . ."—he cleared his throat portentously, and his tone became severe, as though his son-in-law were at that moment standing humbly before him and listening to his oration—". . . and when he arrives, I shall give him a piece of my mind!"

"You're right! You're absolutely right! I was wrong, I confess. I'll accept whatever punishment you order," Hulk whispered, nodding his head vigorously. Then the old man changed the subject yet again: "I have some words for you as well, Aying. Wasn't it partly your fault that he had to get the money behind your back? The most obedient cat steals fish when it's hungry—how can you expect a man to be different? Raising rabbits is a fine thing to do, and if you'd given him the money for it in the first place, he wouldn't have needed to pawn your pants! I think there's a simple solution to the problem: you give him the money to get your pants back, and tell him he can keep the rabbits."

"But Dad," Aying protested, "last time . . . the beetles. . . ."

"If your grandfather dies at the start of the year, that doesn't mean he's going to keep dying year in, year out, does it?" Her father reasoned, potato head on the move once more. "You only have the one grandfather!"

"Dad, you're talking nonsense!" Aying snorted, but there was a smile on her tear-stained face.

"Life and death are written in the stars; riches and fame are ordained by fate." Her father repeated the old nostrum for the umpteenth time, and his head swiveled earnestly: "Riches and fame are ordained by fate, and I've a feeling Hulk is going to get lucky this time. Everyone's being encouraged to go in for moneymaking ventures these days, so Hulk's in step with the times . . . ."

"Can't they change?" Aying interrupted.

"They may, but don't ask me to guess when," he replied with an inscrutable smile.

"Nobody else is keeping rabbits." Aying was still dubious.

"Silly girl, do you want to see the fish before you start to weave your nets?" Her father assumed a look of profound wisdom commensurate with his years. "If he'd been a bit quicker getting started on the beetles, he wouldn't have lost money on them. There's hope for you this time precisely because nobody else is raising rabbits. The proverb says, 'Success with heaven stands; the plans are in men's hands.' It's all in the planning—you're better getting a head start than sitting at home waiting for things to change. . . ."

He followed this up with a great deal more in the same vein, which Hulk couldn't be bothered listening to. He knew all he needed to know—the threat of divorce was over, and his father-in-law was in favor of the rabbits. He wanted to rush in and hug the dear old man. He did no such thing, of course; he just heaved a sigh of relief and patted his son's large head: "Go in, and tell your mother to come home." Then he turned and called softly, "Home, Lazybones! Let's go!"

Lazybones bounded off gleefully. The old man was right: plans are in men's hands. And Hulk had plans.

—7—

In days of peace, some men show their wisdom by writing great books, others by making strategic connections and flattering the powerful. Hulk's own particular genius found its expression in the nurturing of living creatures.

Other people kept rabbits cooped up together like chickens,

but Hulk made eight separate hutches in two stories for his. This wasn't his invention—he'd got some schoolchildren to read him the manual that came with the rabbits and had made his hutches according to its instructions. The manual said that if you kept the rabbits apart, they couldn't bite each other; that way their fur would stay clean and fetch a better price. Everyone who saw Hulk's hutches was struck by their innovative design. Though he'd used only simple strips of bamboo to build them, each hutch was provided with its own dining and toilet facilities. The dining area was a wicker basket attached to the front of the hutch, out of which the little dears could nibble their feed; the toilet was a concrete slab at the back, set at an angle so that the urine and droppings would run away. Hulk washed the concrete slabs daily, like some city dweller rinsing his chamber pot. That way the hutches were always spick and span.

Every morning, Hulk's first action would be to go down to the river and cut a basket of fresh grass, which he would bring straight back to the hutches. The eight little rabbits, as sensitive to his presence as Lazybones, would scamper out at the sound of his step; eight pairs of dainty ears would prick up, and the eyes beneath would gleam. Some of the rabbits would scrabble on their doors with their front paws; others would thump with their hind legs. Hulk would smile as he had in the days when he watched the infant Amao straining to suck at his mother's breast, feeling the same contentment and fulfillment.

After he had divided the food between the wicker baskets on the doors of the hutches, he would watch happily as the rabbits nibbled at the tender grasses through the bamboo slats. His own mouth would start to nibble in sympathy, as though he were himself tasting honey or candy. The soft sound of their chewing was like a light rain nourishing his soul, and his swarthy face would crinkle in a tender smile. They were so sweet, so frail, so pure, and so lovable. The slightest of pinches, and their lives would melt away like a first snowfall. But

Hulk's caresses were light and gentle. His hand was like a great shovel, but it was never clumsy when cupped to hold them, and his callused fingers were full of love as he stroked them.

Hulk's devotion to the rabbits made Lazybones jealous. Glowering, the dog squatted off to one side and growled to remind Hulk that he was still there. Hulk understood the dog's feelings. He called him over and hugged him. Then he lifted one of Lazybones' front paws up to the hutches: "Come on now, shake hands, be friends. We'll have no bullying from now on." Lazybones returned this affection to the full, licking his master's hand and arm as he sniffed at the dainty little creatures. From that time, the dog and the rabbits really did become good friends. Lazybones stood on guard at the hutches, a suitable job for him now that he was getting older and wasn't up to hunting. If one of the doors swung open and a rabbit hopped out, he would snap and send it back home, without ever biting or scratching.

As the rabbits matured, their fur grew thick and fine, soft and white. At the first shearing, Hulk made twenty yuan. Twenty yuan may not be a fortune, but it caused quite a stir in the village. Hulk's house became a hive of activity, with visitors coming through at all hours. Aying found herself brewing tea twice a day and serving pounds of sunflower seeds to all their visitors. She bustled about cheerfully, tirelessly repeating, "The man at the depot said the price was a bit low because this was a first cut—in the future we should be able to make five or six yuan per rabbit each time!"

Hulk was a hero in the village. Everyone called him a maestro for the way he had raised the rabbits and built his hutches. Implicit in this praise, of course, was the request that he bear them in mind when baby rabbits were born. Hulk accepted their praise and requests with magnanimity. Three months later, after the second shearing, he took his five does to be mated. That was when he discovered that the real maestros were the people at the breeding center. Not only did they have beautiful hutches, but they also had hung on each of them a bit of paper with loopy foreign writing. This reminded Hulk of the pair of pants he had bought for Aying, which had had just such a label attached. He concluded that everything of real value must have a label and that bits of paper like these would be certain to raise the value of his rabbits.

Yes indeed, his rabbits must be labeled, too. In fact, he remembered that they had all had little cards when he bought them, but since he had not understand what the cards said, he had taken them off and tucked them carefully into his wife's comb box, along with the label from the pants.

"When the babies are born, they'll need cards too," said the man at the breeding center when the does were mated. Cards were those bits of paper, he decided. But what were they for? What did they mean? Humbly he asked the man for instruction.

"You got the manual, didn't you? It's all in there." With that he returned to his work. Hulk didn't like to pursue the matter, so he packed up his does and went home.

He hadn't realized there was anything about cards in the manual. It wasn't his fault: the children who'd read it for him hadn't been able to make it out, so they'd skipped it, which was only to be expected. So when Hulk got home, he retrieved the bits of paper from his wife's comb box. On the labels was the inscription "WG\R\103." In hopes of finding out what these hieroglyphics meant, he bought a package of brightly colored candied fruit and shared it out among a group of schoolchildren, in return for which they were supposed to explain it all to him. There were as many interpretations offered as there were people; finally a couple of the kids furrowed their brows and read it out loud: "Wu-ge-er. . . ."

"What's *wu-ge-er?*" asked Hulk, none the wiser. They all shrugged helplessly. One of them had an idea: "You should go ask the principal; he knows everything, and he can read anything. Even our teacher has to ask him things sometimes."

The principal was the college boy of years past and Hulk felt a little uncomfortable as he recalled how he had harangued him. Still he steeled himself and went along. The college boy appeared to bear him no grudge; he explained painstakingly that *WG* meant "West Germany," *R* meant "rabbit," and *103* meant that these were the third generation of West German Angoras. Their babies would be 104, fourth generation; and when those bred, the offspring would be 105, fifth generation. The cards were an indication of pedigree so that customers could be assured they were buying the genuine article. Without cards, people might suspect that the rabbits weren't purebred, and that would be a problem.

After giving this explanation, the college boy inscribed a number of cards "WG\R\104" for him to hang on the cages of the new babies. Hulk followed the college boy's instructions precisely. As he did so, he pondered the strangeness of the world. Here was a man who had never raised a rabbit in his life, yet he could wax eloquent on the subject of rabbits simply by looking at a card; and here was Hulk, caring for rabbits day in, day out, with hardly a word to say for himself. Learning wasn't as useless as he had thought; maybe the patch of sky over the college boy was bigger than his own, even if it had been hidden by clouds for a while.

When summer ended, Hulk enrolled his son in school and took him to pay his respects to the college boy. Hulk felt that, with learning, his son might have a larger patch of the sky.

Hulk's own patch of the sky brightened considerably that autumn. The labels on the newest hutches read "WG\R\105," and he had over sixty rabbits. He had already made over two hundred yuan from the sale of their fur. The villagers all complimented him: "Things are looking up for you, Hulk!" "You've struck it rich, Hulk!" Those who hadn't been prepared to part with twenty yuan for the rabbits at the outset were now ready to pay fifty for Hulk's, which they knew to be of good stock, each with a label authenticating its pedigree.

Hulk reflected that when he had bought the rabbits for twenty a pair, he had never suspected that he would be selling them for fifty. Actually, thirty a pair would have been plenty—even at that price, twenty or thirty of the newborns would bring in two or three hundred yuan. Over lunch he suggested to Aying that they invite a few potential customers around to view the rabbits.

As ever, Aying disagreed. She pouted: "We're not selling! You're like a rat that won't leave itself any food to eat later. Use your head: the 105s will be breeding in a couple of months, eight to a litter, and the next lot in another six months. Eight eights are sixty-four—keep it up for a year, and how many will you have? How much fur will you be shearing? We won't need to do farmwork at all. We'll be pulling in a thousand a year from the fur, and we'll be able to build our new house!"

There was something in what his wife said, but Hulk still wanted to sell a few. "It's okay to let other people have them," he said, scratching his head. "Otherwise they'll be jealous of us, and that would make them feel bad."

Aying snorted: "Have you forgotten how they treated you?" Naturally Hulk remembered all too clearly how wretched he had felt in the days when he had been criticized and forced to cut off his dog's tail, nor had he forgotten his misery when others made money on the ground beetles and he'd lost everything. But why should he impose hardship on others just because he had suffered himself? He found this idea hard to explain, especially to his wife. So he just sighed: "People need to be at peace."

It didn't seem to bother Aying whether Hulk was at peace or not. After lunch she locked up the rabbit shed, put the key in her patent-leather bag, and took Amao off for a visit to her father.

Hulk paced up and down in frustration, but there wasn't a thing he could do. People came by throughout the afternoon, but the rabbits were locked up in their cages like zoo animals, barely visible through the bars. Hulk felt that he had lost face—it was only recently that face had been important to him—so he lied, and said that his wife had taken the key with her by mistake, and invited them all to come round some other time.

Had this kind of thing happened before, there would have been a barrage of abuse directed at Hulk, which would have left him tongue-tied. Now there were no hard words, and everyone professed themselves quite willing to come back later. The team leader even slapped him on the back: "Keep up the good work, Hulk. There's someone from the commune radio station coming to interview you in a few days, so we'll all be hearing about you on the air."

Laughing and chattering, the visitors left. Hulk locked the house and headed off, Lazybones at his heels. As he looked over fields shrouded with evening mist, a wry smile appeared on his face: "It's just you and me again, old friend!"

It's hard to be a man. People quarrel when they're poor, and now he and Aying were at odds because they were getting rich. Thank heavens he had such a wonderful man for a father-in-law. That was perhaps the greatest blessing of all. If it hadn't been for him, who knows what might have become of them? To Hulk, the old man was something of a saint. Without his saintliness, how could Hulk and Aying have stayed together through the bad times? Not that Hulk was always sure what the old man was talking about, especially when he started rotating his balding pate and pronouncing on "the wisdom of the sages of yore." But what did that matter? The old man had read so many profound books that he had to be talking sense. Still, what about this time? If he were on Hulk's side, then there would be no need to say anything, but what if he disagreed? Father-in-Law couldn't be ignored! If they didn't sell any rabbits, Hulk could live with the loss of face, but what if someone decided to cut off the tails of capitalism again? What if the market for rabbits collapsed? Then again, rabbits are sensitive creatures—they might all be wiped out by disease; if they survived, they might even run off without a trace. Hulk knew all this from previous experience raising rabbits for the table. His heart began to pound.

But even with a pounding heart, he didn't feel anywhere near as bad as he had the last time. He had, after all, made a success of rabbits, he could stand tall, and there was no threat of divorce.

For some reason he thought of the saying about "blowing your own horn," and it amused him mightily. People are strange—one minute they treat you like a piece of shit, the next you're Superman. Just as the college boy had suddenly made good again, so Hulk might yet have another chance to play the big shot as he had when he was a poor-peasant representative. Mind you, being a big shot was all very well, but was it worth tempting providence and risking condemnation again?

Perplexed, he looked up at the heavens. The sun had just set, and the sky was an opaque gray. The moon had not yet risen, but a few early stars twinkled faintly. He thought back to a day in his childhood. He was lying on a bamboo mat in the doorway to keep cool. His head resting on his hands, he gazed up at the mass of stars that filled the heavens. The stars were packed tightly together, some bright like golden ears of corn, some faint as specks of dust. "Ma," he asked, "why are there so many stars in the sky?"

"There's a star up there for everyone on earth." His mother fanned herself as she answered. "There are some whose luck is good, and they have stars the size of grain bins. Others, the ill-fated ones, theirs are smaller than the beards of barley."

"Which is your star, Ma?"

"Mine is a speck of chaff, too small to be seen."

As she spoke, a beautiful golden light streaked through the sky and vanished. He trembled: "What was that, Ma?"

"That was a shooting star," she replied, "and when children

see one of those, they should close their eyes and recite the name of Amithaba Buddha because it means that someone has just died."

He didn't say the Buddha's name, but he stared long and hard at the vault of heaven, upset at his inability to see his mother's star.

Now a thought flashed through his brain like a shooting star: Didn't his mother's words mean much the same as what his father-in-law was always saying? Everything was ordained —your star might be as big as a grain bin or as small as chaff, but whichever it was, it was destined. The old man had an inscription above the door: "Comprehend the order of the universe, and your spirit will be at peace." How true! A man's spirit needs to be at peace. Look at Hulk—he had suffered, eating tree roots in the years of natural disaster and cutting off his dog's tail in the campaign against capitalism, but he'd survived, hadn't he? Why look for trouble now he was doing so well with the rabbits? As to whether the bottom would fall out of the market or whether there would be more cutting off of capitalist tails, it was written in the stars, and there was no point getting upset about it.

Never, he felt, had his heart and his father-in-law's been so in harmony. Every word the old man had said came back to him now, each one more precious than gold or jewels. Had Hulk been an educated man he would have averred that they were pearls of irrefutable wisdom, the cornerstones of the national tradition, the distillation of moral virtue. Such sentiments were, of course, beyond his powers of articulation, but nevertheless he felt that a sublime light was shining on him. He was at peace. He was confident that his father-in-law would take his side.

"Lazybones!" he called happily. At that moment, a ferocious-looking black hunting dog appeared from behind a pile of dirt by the road. In the fading light, Hulk saw to his amazement that this dog also had a stump instead of a tail. He stared at the dog and then, unable to control his curiosity, called out to the dog's owner, "Hey, mate, was your dog a capitalist too?"

"You crazy?" The owner, a thickset man of middle age, glowered at him. "I'm third-generation peasant, genuine proletarian class!"

"Then why's he got no tail?" Hulk looked at the black dog. "Mine's that way because I had to cut off his capitalist tail."

The man finally understood what Hulk was talking about, and he burst out laughing: "Call yourself a hunter, sonny? Think you know about hunting dogs?" Hulk started to nod, but then he changed his mind and shook his head. He wasn't really that much of a hunter—his ancestors had tilled the soil for generations, and he was the first one who had even considered hunting for a living.

The man walked up to Hulk, laughed long and loud, and clapped him on the back: "Sonny, all hunting dogs are bobtailed. Proletarian or capitalist, they all have their tails docked when they're pups so they'll be more agile when they grow up."

Hulk was so delighted with this explanation that he almost jumped for joy. He felt deeply satisfied. The criticism of capitalism really had been brilliant and timely after all—if not for that campaign, he'd never have dreamed of cutting off the tail of his beloved Lazybones. And if he hadn't cut it off then but waited till all the bones had hardened, how much more painful it would have been! It seemed as though Lazybones too had his little patch of sky, and perhaps he also had his own tiny star in the great firmament of the night! If Hulk's patch of sky were put beside Lazybones', then it would be that much greater; if their stars were side by side, the light would be that much brighter.

Without a care in the world, Hulk strode cheerfully along the path that led to his father-in-law's cottage.

The Festival of Graves

—1—

Rain beat down, relentless and slate-gray in the howling wind. It poured through the bare branches of the trees and battered the stunted shoots of winter wheat. Only the shallow river rejoiced, as it swallowed up the rain and the turbid streams that swept along the ditches between the fields. Then the wind died down, and the rain stopped. Sunlight pierced the clouds like a magic sword, and the land shone. The river waters rushed on in shining torrents, sweeping away the waterweeds left behind from the year before.

The trill of a bird wafted from the depths of the bamboo grove, breaking the silence of winter. But people seemed unconvinced by this harbinger of spring, until they looked up at the soft blue of the sky or noticed pale yellow buds of forsythia on the sunlit slopes and shepherd's purse spreading its carpet of fresh white flowers over the fields.

Wind followed, then more rain and a rumble of thunder. After the storm subsided, the sun broke through again, and a profusion of lilac wolfberries, yellow dandelions, and blue wildflowers dotted the meadows like stars. An emerald curtain of weeping willow fronds adorned with tiny catkins of pastel yellow billowed to the surface of the water.

She surveyed it all coldly, and the stirring of new life filled her with an irrational dread. Each day the earth became more bountiful, and each day she felt more empty and alone. Here it was again, April Fifth, the Festival of Graves. Withered branches along the riverside thrust forth buds of white and red, peach and plum trees burst into bloom, and in the vegetable plots the rape plants flowered golden yellow. Bamboo shoots pushed like steer horns through the soil, and the leaves on the willow trees burst forth like blossoms. The waterweeds revived and embellished the waters with their vivid color. When she opened the door, a dazzling haze of green confronted her.

As she brushed her hair, she examined herself in the mirror. She saw a gray, lined face, eyes like dry wells, a sharp nose, and a puckered mouth. Worst of all was her chin, which looked as if it had been gouged away by a shovel. Her few remaining teeth protruded between thin lips. It was the face of an old woman ready for the coffin.

Try as she might, she couldn't understand how age had crept up on her. Other women could watch their children grow and sigh at the passage of time: "They're so big now, it's no wonder I'm getting on." But there was none of this for Huang Huizhen, she who had handled women's affairs and served as the commune's Party secretary. She had not endured the pain of childbirth or known the joy and pride of being a mother and grandmother. Her life seemed to have jumped from childhood to old age; the fantasies of young womanhood had hardly existed. The past was reduced to a dim vision: the setting sun burning out like a last ember in the ashes, the moon's pale crescent high in an inky sky. An old graybeard emerged from the gloom, singing a senseless riddle:

"From times gone by, who knows when,
few survive three score and ten.
Childhood slips by in a haze,
dotage passes in a daze.

In between is haste and hurry,
days of toil and nights of worry.
Once mid-autumn's come and gone,
see the moon grow pale and wan.
Past the Festival of Graves,
flowers wither, blossoms fade . . ."

She must have been six years old, squatting by a stream playing in the mud, kneading crumbs of soil into the shape of rolls, then crumbling them and starting again. The strange song had delighted her then. She looked up to catch a glimpse of the old man's face, but just then the last dim light of dusk died. Disembodied, the gruff voice sang on:

"Round and round the seasons go,
the curfew tolls, the roosters crow. . . ."

There had been more besides, but she couldn't remember what. Something about grave mounds, perhaps. Nor could she remember who the old graybeard was. An uncle, maybe a great-uncle—at any rate someone from her family. It embarrassed her that not all her ancestors had been the simple commoners she would have liked them to be.

Huang Huizhen couldn't understand why this vision had been haunting her since the beginning of spring. Why should she be remembering the events of childhood so late in life? At times she felt she had dreamed it all. The graybeard couldn't possibly be any relation of hers. How could she, a Communist, a revolutionary, and a materialist, indulge in such delusions? Why could she not recall the deeds from her past that merited praise and brought her glory? Was this some ill omen, warning her that she was not long for the world?

She was a little afraid of dying. She was already sixty-six years old, and as the local saying goes, "Sixty-six, sixes doubling, bean curd boiling hot and bubbling." This means that when you get to this age, the traditional funeral dish of bean curd is ready for your death. So the custom of the region was for all daughters to give their parents sixty-six cubes of pork on the Festival of Graves in the year they reached sixty-six. It was said that by eating the sixty-six cubes of meat the old folks could avoid illness. Then, once this milestone had been passed, the parents could live on for many more years. So, on this morning, people who had survived into their sixty-sixth year would all wait anxiously for their daughters to come by. Those who had no daughter of their own would make arrangements for a stand-in, who would carefully prepare a bowl of diced pork and carry it ostentatiously through the village.

Huang Huizhen would not copy the practices of ignorant peasants. She was a woman of status and high revolutionary consciousness and had always despised such customs as adopting stand-in daughters and eating sixty-six pieces of pork. She also knew something about science and realized that for older people to eat so much meat at a single sitting could be hard on their systems and certainly would not prolong their lives. Besides, there was the expense to be considered! Such cogent reasoning should have been enough to reassure her, but somehow it did not. How unfathomable people can be—sometimes we can see into everyone's heart but our own.

On the morning of the Festival of Graves, she was ill at ease. Outside, spring was bright and fecund, so much so that the festival to honor the dead became a celebration of life. The villagers were making the sticky-rice dumplings that are always eaten at the festival, kneading them into all sorts of shapes, round, elongated, and pointed. Pampered children took bites out of each kind. If they did not like what they tasted, they would spit it out, or else they would eat the filling and discard the slippery outer shells. Grandmothers would grumble at their antics, but even when the little darlings tossed their leftovers to the chickens and ducks or played with them like mud pies, it didn't seem to affect the general good mood.

In Huang Huizhen's eyes, these unlettered rustics were no

better than mother hens sitting on their eggs. All they cared about was raising sons and carrying on the family line. All these years after the revolution, their consciousness was still so low that they were more concerned about the yield from their beans or the fact that their latest grandchild had a dick than they were about the great affairs of the Party and the state. She found this vexing and painful. Huang Huizhen would not pander to their primitive beliefs or join in their merriment.

She looked silently round at her four walls, hung with the pictures of her past. There had been a time when she had liked to open the windows and flood the room with light, letting the sun's crimson rays shine on her photographs and warm her heart. But later she had become nervous about drafts, and the windows had remained shut tight from that time on. Now the photographs before her were yellowing and faded with age.

The damp cold chilled her to the bone. She had lived alone since her husband's death, without even a dog or a chicken to keep her company. Now the place seemed uninhabited, a wasteland, with no babies crying, children toddling, and toys scattered about.

There was a measured knocking at the door. Startled, she sat bolt upright. Then, after a moment, the knocking came again, still firm, and courteously insistent. She hurried to her feet, her heart fluttering with hope. Could it possibly be . . . had her daughter come?

For she had a daughter. Not her own flesh and blood, but the child of her husband's first wife. Even though she was a stepmother, she had truly loved the child and cared for her. When the girl was young, she had taught her to sing, "The sky in the liberated areas is the brightest sky of all," and told her tales of the Red Army's final surge to victory in the civil war. She wasn't one to coddle a child, but she certainly never treated her poorly. There had always been food on the table and clothes to wear. Not too many clothes, of course, and not much in the way of treats and toys, but what harm was there in raising the child in the tradition of revolutionary austerity? When her daughter married, she gave her two chests and some quilts as her dowry. What the girl actually wanted was a dressing table, but Huang Huizhen drew the line at that. Dressing tables were for the pampered young daughters of the bourgeoisie. How could a Communist Party cadre provide such a gift? When she saw how disappointed her daughter was, she spent a little extra on books; but the young couple seemed uninterested in the kind of books she gave them and behaved most ungratefully. They did maintain appearances, however, and visited her at New Year and on festivals.

Her daughter became pregnant soon after the wedding and gave birth to a little girl. The young woman, her husband, and his parents all wanted to try again for a boy. By then, however, the one-child policy was in effect, and Huang Huizhen was the official responsible for women's matters. She tried several times to persuade her daughter to volunteer for sterilization, but the young woman would not consent and began to avoid her. So Huang Huizhen went to the factory where her daughter worked and impressed on them that they were not to make any concessions in this case because of connections with officialdom. Her daughter's response was to stop going in to work. Six months later there was a general inspection by the birth control authorities, and all the women of the commune were ordered to present themselves for examination. Huang Huizhen's daughter was brought in, already heavily pregnant. The mother's face darkened with fury: "Take her away, and abort it!" Guards stepped forward to drag her away, but the young woman slumped to the ground and wailed, "Mother, Mother, I beg you, let me have my baby!"

Huang Huizhen remembered her daughter as a headstrong child, too proud to beg, who had seldom called her Mother. So she was quite taken aback at such desperate pleading. Still, birth control was Party work, and how could she let personal feelings interfere with that? If she let her daughter off, how could she enforce the policy on other women?

When they heard that Huang Huizhen had refused to give permission for the baby to be born, her son-in-law and his parents, both of them in their sixties, came in and knelt before her. "Chief Huang," begged the old grandfather, "if you'll only let her give birth, the whole family will kowtow and burn incense for you, and the child will remember your kindness all his life. . . ."

Huang Huizhen was exasperated at their pigheadedness and hissed through clenched teeth, "All right, if you want the child so much, pay the fine. It's a thousand yuan!"

In fact, the regulations stipulated half that. She had spoken as she had only to get rid of them since she was sure they couldn't raise the cash. But, instead, her words seemed to galvanize them all like a shot of ginseng. They dashed off to borrow what they needed, and within twelve hours they were back to her with the thousand yuan. Not that it did them any good. Huang Huizhen was the kind of official who always has to take the lead in implementing Party policy and never invites the disapproval of her superiors. She refused the money, and her daughter was hauled off to the clinic. An examination confirmed that she was seven months pregnant, and an abortion was ordered. But then—and nobody quite knew how it could have been done with so many watching eyes—someone slipped her a note, and she announced that she had to go to the bathroom. Guards were sent with her, of course, and posted at the door. But when after several minutes she had still not emerged, they went in to find the room empty! Incredibly she had managed, as heavily pregnant as she was, to escape through a high and narrow window.

There must have been accomplices! It was a conspiracy! Huang Huizhen was livid. Her husband attempted to talk her around as they lay in bed that night: the girl was his only family, and besides she was seven months gone; why not just let her have the child? Such talk only made her more determined, and after a sleepless night she sent people out at daybreak to tie her daughter up and bring her in.

They strapped her to the birthing table and induced labor. To the astonishment of all, the seven-month fetus was alive—and a boy! The doctor had no choice but to put the baby in an incubator. The daughter's whole family was overjoyed: they lit incense, recited the name of the Buddha, and then came happily along to pay the fine. The hospital officials were at a loss to know what they should do, so they went to Huang Huizhen to ask for directions. Huang Huizhen ordered them to remove the baby from the incubator immediately. Shortly after, his little life ebbed away.

Her daughter's family wailed in anguish. Mad with rage, the old father-in-law seized a knife and vowed to have it out with Huang Huizhen. If the authorities hadn't intervened, locking the old man up for a few months on a charge of intended homicide, her life might have been at risk.

The ill will that this incident had generated between her daughter and herself had endured for over ten years. Her daughter had never visited her since then. The consensus of the village gossips was that Huang had gone too far. People felt that she had only been so mean because the girl wasn't her own flesh and blood. But that just wasn't so! It wasn't that there was any bad blood between her and her daughter. She was acting for the Party and the state, for the public good!

Time and time again she had considered going to see her daughter to explain, but the girl had become a stranger to her. Only today did she realize how much she longed to see her again. She shook convulsively as she reached for the doorknob. Today is the festival, she thought. Perhaps my daughter will bring me sixty-six pieces of pork like the village bumpkins do. . . .

But when she opened the door, it was to a messenger to tell

her that she should go to county headquarters for a Party meeting.

Despite her disappointment, she felt some slight comfort. At least officialdom hadn't forgotten her. Even if her daughter didn't bring her anything, the county would treat her to a meal—and a few pieces of pork would be nothing compared to the banquet that was certain to follow the meeting.

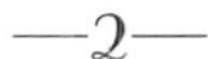

It was mild outside, the warm breeze redolent with pollen and honey. On this day, the Festival of Graves, there was an unaccustomed bustle of activity by the bend in the river where the commune's dead rested. For many years, the graves had been neglected and allowed to become overgrown, their only visitors passing birds pecking at the nut bush. The dead had passed lonely years in the shadows of solemn evergreens, secure in their coffins, spared the atrocities that the living committed against each other. Now, however, times were changing. In a period of affluence, people were more inclined to feel concern for their ancestors, and on this festival day they brought offerings of fish and meat, wine and vegetables, to the gravesides. Now that they had more to spend on themselves, they worried that the dead might still be poor, so they burned silver ingots made of tinfoil. Strings of paper money, yellow, white, and green, hung from the trees by the graves, spinning in the breeze like colored lights revolving over a dance floor. Huang Huizhen had always turned up her nose at such superstition, but today she was a little less inclined to find fault.

She was quite warm by the time she arrived at the government office compound. Sweat beaded on the tip of her nose, and her cheeks were flushed as if she had been drinking. Other old comrades were streaming in to attend the meeting. Some were being led along by their grandchildren, some were perched on the backs of bicycles pedaled by their sons, still others hobbled in leaning on their canes. In this company, Huang Huizhen seemed very sprightly to have come along under her own steam.

She had every reason to feel proud of herself. She had served a three-year term as Party secretary of the commune (or county, as it was now called). The two pines at the gate of the compound had been planted in those years on her orders. Since then, an orchard had been added, which shimmered with the pink petals of flowering cherries—trees that to her eyes were eminently lacking in the resolute spirit of the pines. In her days . . . but enough of that. Her back was straight and her head held high as she strode into the meeting hall.

Through force of habit, she surveyed the room as she entered. Nobody jumped up and exclaimed, "Here's Secretary Huang!" Nobody ran over with a stool or poured her a cup of tea. It was as if she, their former Party secretary, were invisible to them, like a bubble, like thin air. They just sat there chattering merrily away, gossiping or complaining about their sons and daughters-in-law. Irritated at their rudeness, she cleared her throat. At last some of them looked around at her, nodded briefly, forced a smile, and then went back to discussing all the things they had to do at home and comparing their various aches and pains.

She stalked angrily over to a seat by the window, sat down, and did her best to ignore them. Of course she wouldn't join in—here they were, old Party members, hardly out of office, and they had turned into a pack of gossips. What a disgrace! She wouldn't have tolerated this kind of sloppiness when she was Party secretary. But the new deputy county head didn't seem bothered by it at all. He read through a Party document about carrying out rectification at the local level with a smug grin on his face and then remarked to the chattering crowd in front of him, "Well, now I've put you in the know about the spirit of the document from Party Central. Considering the fact that you're all getting on, and it's been quite an effort for you to make it to county headquarters today, I suggest that you have your lunch and then head home."

Huang Huizhen had understood perfectly well when she was summoned to county headquarters that the meeting would be only a formality. Still, she was most displeased at what this wet-behind-the-ears official had to say. In her day, whenever Party Central had announced a new initiative or set forth key duties, she never failed to organize discussion groups and send feedback to her superiors. Then she would select model peasants for everyone else to emulate, identify pacesetters in carrying out the new policy, and publicize their experience with the campaign. And what did you get these days? "Put you in the know," indeed! "Have some lunch!" What do you take us old comrades for? Are we just windbags, lunch buckets? Others might be willing to accept it, but not Huang Huizhen. She had joined the Party in 1948, before this new deputy county head had been born.

Not that she didn't want the meal, of course. After the exertions of the morning, she had started to feel hungry some time ago. Besides, one of her reasons for coming was that she wanted to eat meat, to make up for her disappointment over the sixty-six cubes of pork.

The meeting hall was transformed into a dining hall, and young Butch, the chef from the county government offices, came in with some other youngsters to lay out the bowls and chopsticks. She couldn't abide Butch. His class origins weren't anything to be proud of, and to make matters worse, he followed current fashions, growing his hair long like a girl, wearing jeans that hugged his backside, and talking in slang that didn't sound at all proper. He also took advantage of the fact that he and the new chief had gone to school together and had been roommates when they had returned to the village. Now he addressed the deputy county head unceremoniously as

"Little Li." And not only did the official allow this, but he even slapped the other on the back: "Hey, buddy, mind how you do your work today. Cook the meat as tender as you can; these old comrades don't chew so well."

Butch was downright rude. Staring maliciously right at Huang Huizhen, he snorted: "Huh, they've eaten well so long they've all rotted their teeth." Little Li merely slapped him on the back to shut him up: "Cut the crap, eh?"

Butch pulled a face and went off to another table. The deputy county head didn't pursue the matter, just turned to address the gathering: "Since the meal isn't ready yet, why don't you old comrades make some suggestions about how the county administration should do its work in the future?"

This lackadaisical attitude made Huang Huizhen's blood boil. What kind of a Party leader was he? Consorting with hooligans, even putting the children of landlords and rich peasants in positions of responsibility! Where were the prestige and principles of a Communist Party member? She couldn't stand it any longer. Her face puffed, and purple with rage, she rose abruptly.

"Since we're in a Party rectification," she snapped, "I'll be blunt. Our present leadership is short on Party spirit, it lacks principles, and its political standards are low."

The listeners looked at each other nervously, unsure of how to react. Working herself up even more, she picked a newspaper up off the table, rolled it up, and slapped the table with it: "When I was doing underground work, I was under the leadership of the comrades who had come south to fight the civil war, and in those days. . . ."

Everyone was silent. They had heard this line from Huang Huizhen almost daily when she had been Party secretary. She had only to mention coming south, and you knew a lecture would follow; like it or not, you had to pay attention, or you were in big trouble! This time, however, after a few seconds of bemused silence, there were snorts of laughter. Amid the laughter someone muttered, "Huh, coming south with the leaders of the Red Army! I've heard that some of those women were sold into whorehouses and they haven't come out yet!" Someone else added, "What do the old whores think they have to brag about?" It was just as well the laughter was so loud and that Huang Huizhen didn't hear the last few words, or she might really have had a fit. As it was, she was so furious her mind was a blur. If it had just been the common people being so impudent, she could have borne it, but these were Party cadres! All of them had always been subservient and attentive to her, and now they were mocking her brazenly. Could the inconceivable be true—that their behavior toward her in the past was all a sham? At a momentary loss for words, she opened the newspaper in her hand and saw the bold print of a headline: "PARTY GENERAL SECRETARY VISITS EUROPE." There was a photograph beside the report. As she looked at it, the blood rushed to her head. She gesticulated and shouted, "Don't you laugh! I've got criticisms of the general secretary as well! He's leader of the Party, but instead of doing rectification work, he's off on a trip overseas. That's the job of the foreign minister. . . ."

Before she could finish, the tension broke, and the listeners began to howl with laughter. Butch called out for someone to rub his stomach and ease the pain of laughing. The laughter was so loud it threatened to blow the roof off. The new deputy county head hurriedly gestured them all to lay off: "Don't laugh, folks. A Party member has a right to air her opinions about the leadership."

He was trying to keep a straight face, but everyone could tell from the twinkle in his eye and the catch in his voice that he couldn't completely suppress his mirth. Butch found it hard to contain himself as well, but muttering "crazy bitch!" and rubbing his belly, he headed back into the kitchen: "Hey guys, here's a newsflash, April fifth, New China News Agency! They've dug up a mummy from the tombs at Mawangdui who wants to take a potshot at the Central Committee!"

His young fellow workers clustered round: "What do you mean?"

Butch couldn't resist the opportunity to do an impersonation. By the time he was through, everyone else was holding their sides as well. Then Butch shook his head and said more soberly, "It's hard to understand why, but they get old, and the brain starts to go. Oh, yes, I almost forgot—Little Li said to cook the stuff soft or the old monkeys won't be able to chew it."

An old cook who was chopping meat on the table broke in: "What's so hard to understand? You shouldn't make fun of her. In the old days, you'd have been called a rightist or a counterrevolutionary for less than that!"

There was menace in his voice, but Butch's assistants were just a bunch of kids, without any understanding of what the words *rightist* and *counterrevolutionary* meant. They just laughed at the old cook as if he, too, were some ancient relic.

The old man saw how little they respected his experience, so he pointed to Butch: "You don't believe me? His father talked too much, and that was the end of him!"

That wiped the smile from Butch's face. His father had been framed and sentenced to labor reform in a coal mine, where he had been killed when a mine shaft had caved in. The case had been determined by Huang Huizhen, which was why Butch had always loathed her. He had been a child when his father died, and his mother had not had the education to explain the whys and wherefores of the case to her son. Thus it was still a mystery to him why Huang Huizhen had taken it on herself to brand his father a counterrevolutionary. Now that the old cook had raised the subject, Butch asked him what had happened.

"It's a long story," said the old man. "It was during the

Great Leap Forward in 1958, and Huang Huizhen's husband —he was the boss of the co-op in those days—told everyone to plant five hundred catties of seed on every mu of land and harvest a hundred thousand catties of grain from it. If you try to spread that many seeds onto a single mu, they'll rot, and most won't sprout. Huang Huizhen was pretty ingenious, though. She mobilized the entire village to paint old newspapers with paste, then stick the seeds onto it standing on their ends. When the newspapers were loaded with seeds, they laid them down in the fields and covered them with soil. . . ."

This had them all baffled. Someone asked, "Did they really plant their fields that way? Did the seeds grow?"

"Sure," the old cook nodded, "a couple of shoots here and there, nothing more."

Butch was beginning to understand where the story was leading, but the other youngsters still hadn't a clue. In their innocence they asked, "So what's this all got to do with Butch's dad?"

The old cook pushed cubes of meat to the side of the chopping block and continued slowly. "Butch's father was teacher at the primary school at the time, and when there was something nobody else could understand, we would always go to him for an explanation. He said that what Huang Huizhen was doing was against the laws of nature, and he wrote a letter saying so to the authorities. He even sent an article to the newspaper, which was how he came to be dragged away as a counterrevolutionary. Nobody doubted his scientific knowledge. . . ."

The old cook sighed and changed his tone abruptly: "That's all in the past now. Don't let it get you down, Butch. Just try and mind your manners a bit; don't shoot your mouth off all the time. You meddle in things that don't concern you and say things that shouldn't be spoken. Take that business about criticizing the Party general secretary. It's all very well for Huang Huizhen to talk like that, but if you'd breathed a word of it when she was in power, she would have had you tied up and dragged off. Face the facts, we're not all equal, you have to give way. . . . Butch, hey Butch?"

The old man looked around, but Butch was gone. Then he saw him going into the hall bearing a tray loaded with food.

It was a splendid lunch. The pork was as tender as the deputy county head had said it should be, and the chicken was falling from the bone. Butch had divided the food into individual portions and placed the same selection before each of the diners.

Only Huang Huizhen had an extra dish at her place, a bowl decorated with a blue floral design, full to the brim with bubbling white bean curd, fragrant with the tang of green onions, a rich sauce dripping down the side onto the table.

"How come she gets bean curd, and I don't?" complained the person sitting beside her.

Butch sniggered: "Take it easy. Just let her have what she deserves."

Huang Huizhen was starting to feel a little better. The spread before her was eminently superior to sixty-six cubes of pork, and it looked as if she were finally getting some preferential treatment. But when she heard what Butch said, she realized the intent behind the bowl of "bean curd boiling hot and bubbling," and she trembled with rage. "Butch . . . how dare you!"

Butch stood to one side watching her, the tray still in his hands, the corners of his mouth curled in a half smile of malice that made her shiver. Huang Huizhen's face turned from sallow to crimson, then from crimson to white. She slammed down her bowl and stormed out.

How unfair it was! She had lived long enough, she should die now that she was sixty-six, she couldn't take any more of this aggravation! What kind of monster was Butch? How could he humiliate her like that? Just because he was friends with the deputy county head . . . or maybe the deputy county head was behind it all! When the higher-ups had decided a few years ago that he should take over from her, she had put up a stubborn fight—why should they take her power away when she was in good health and prepared to redouble her efforts for the revolution? Besides, how could she relax if her power were handed over to someone like that? A young guy in his thirties, born after she joined the Party! So cocksure of himself because he'd been to college! Always on about incentives and efficiency! Dancing around with a bunch of delinquents! Where would his dance lead them all?

He got the position anyway. Still, as a result of her efforts, he was given only the rank of deputy rather than full county head, as the original plan had been. He must have set up today's scene to get revenge on her.

But Huang Huizhen was still Huang Huizhen. Rattled as she was, she didn't lose control altogether. From her jumble of thoughts, a course of action emerged. She decided she would pay a visit to County Head Zhu.

He wasn't like Little Li. County Head Zhu was a solid cadre of the old school. In years past he had served under Huang Huizhen as office manager for the Party branch office, and she had seen to it that he was designated as one of the next generation of leaders. In her campaign to stop opportunists like Little Li from getting power, she and Office Manager Zhu had busied themselves day and night with their investigations, collected incriminating evidence, called all kinds of meetings, busied themselves till their hair turned gray, and suffered who knows how many sleepless nights!

In the end it had been Zhu who had composed the letter denouncing Little Li. They decided that their letter would have to be anonymous for the time being. This was because Little Li was the cunning type: he knew how to suck up to people, and he always managed to get the credit when things went right and to avoid criticism for disasters.

Naturally the district authorities took the letter very seriously and spent over a year investigating the Little Li affair. But then they ruled that the accusations were largely hearsay and slander. Huang Huizhen was appalled at the decision and upset to think of all the wasted effort. Little Li was delighted and ready to celebrate his promotion. Then, all of a sudden, the policy changed. The top leadership stopped promoting people several grades at once and went back to a system of letting them go up a step at a time. So Little Li rose only to deputy head, while the higher rank—county head and county party secretary—went to the author of the anonymous letter, Office Manager Zhu. Even the darkest of clouds have silver linings after all.

She walked out of county headquarters and followed the road east. In a while she saw the birdcages hanging above the balcony of County Head Zhu's home. Her spirits revived. Zhu was the forthright and generous sort. He would always let her have her pick of his birds. Once he had bought a talking parrot at considerable expense, and, simply because she had admired it, he had sent his wife around with the bird as a gift that very evening.

She should have a good talk with County Head Zhu. Not only did she plan to tell him what she thought of Little Li and offer advice on how he should proceed; she also intended to discuss the great affairs of Party and state. The land in the village was now being contracted out to families, and individuals were being allowed to hire laborers and exploit them. In the cities, foreign capitalists were being invited over to manage factories, entrepreneurs were opening businesses, and there were merchants and peddlers all over the place. The only thing missing from the 1940s were the foreign concessions! No, they even had them, too, though they gave them a slightly nicer name: *special economic zones.* What did all this have to do with socialism! It wasn't just some fit of pique that had made her say she was going to protest about the Party general secretary. But those people . . . they were all cadres who had been nurtured by the Party, yet they were so unfeeling, they had mocked her. . . . Huh, you can laugh! Just remember, she who laughs last laughs longest! Some day the Central Committee would come back to its senses. Her only regret was that since she was getting on in years, sixty-six already, she might not live to see the day. County Head Zhu was younger, though—he'd be around when the time came. But, then again, even he was fifty-eight and unlikely to outlast Little Li. In three years' time, County Head Zhu would be forced into retirement as she had been, and Little Li would take over. That prospect worried her dreadfully. She would have to suggest ways Zhu could make his position more secure.

She hurried on toward County Head Zhu's house. She didn't know whether he would be in, so she peeped in through the high window that faced the road. He was there, so she went up to the door and knocked. Nobody answered at first, so she rapped a little harder and called out, "County Head Zhu, Little Zhu!"

It wasn't Zhu who opened the door but his wife, a forced smile on her face: "Oh, it's you. . . . I'm so sorry, he's . . . he's not at home just now. . . ."

Not at home? But she'd just seen him at the table! At a loss for words, she stared dumbly at the wrinkles etched into the woman's fat face, as if seeking an explanation in the pattern of their lines.

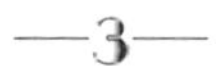

The river flowed quickly that spring. Broken twigs from the past year were whisked around in little whirlpools or swept along by the current. Huang Huizhen realized that fate had been as relentless and unfeeling to her as those cold waters, sweeping away everything that she had been. What had it all been for, her life of struggle? She wasn't so sure anymore. Everyone had forsaken her, her colleagues had humiliated her

. . . no need to dwell on that now. But County Head Zhu, Little Zhu, her protégé, her successor! She had cared for him, guided him along like a younger brother, and now he treated her like a stranger! He was there, she knew he was, but his wife said, "He's not at home"! Just like that—as if she'd been a beggar at his door.

She trudged along in a dream. Or perhaps it was the past that was the dream from which she was now waking. The wind blew chill against her, its cold cutting her heart, and she began to shiver in spite of herself. Yet, oddly enough, the flowers, grasses, and trees seemed to be absorbing warmth from the sun despite the cold and flourished vigorously, growing strong and spirited. Young women stepped out, dressed in their brightest and newest clothes, bearing woven baskets containing sixty-six cubes of pork for their parents. Courting couples strolled along arm in arm, the men in Western suits and leather shoes, the women with their hair flowing free over their shoulders. Huang Huizhen disapproved of all this. It was a scene from another planet to her. And so confusing—had she woken from a dream or returned to one?

Huang Huizhen wavered, not knowing where she should go next. Everything before her was a blur, fields stretching as far as the eye could see, the setting sun fading like a last crimson ember dying in the ashes. High in the blue-black sky, the slender crescent of the pale new moon was rising. Out of the gloom came the old graybeard, singing his senseless riddle:

"From times gone by, who knows when,
few survive three score and ten.
Childhood slips by in a haze,
dotage passes in a daze.
In between is haste and hurry,
days of toil and nights of worry.
Once mid-autumn's come and gone,
see the moon go pale and wan.
Past the Festival of Graves,
flowers wither, blossoms fade. . . . "

She was six again, playing in the mud by the stream, kneading tiny fragments into the shape of rolls, then crumbling them and repeating the process. The strange song enchanted her. She looked up to see the old man's face, but in that instant the last glimmerings of dusk were covered by the curtain of blackness. The desolate sound of the gruff voice continued:

"Round and round the seasons go,
the curfew tolls, the roosters crow.
See your dead before your eyes,
weeds grow yearly where they lie,
Unattended, overgrown,
hosts of grave mounds high and low. . . ."

Now that she had remembered the last couple of lines, she felt a marvelous sense of relief. She saw that she had come to the bend in the river where the graves lay. How could she be here? This wasn't the road home. She was about to turn back when her eye lit on a familiar figure, a woman in a purple jacket, her hair permed, kneeling by a grave with a wicker basket in her hand. It was her daughter. She was lifting dishes out of the basket, making offerings to her father.

As Huang Huizhen watched, a sudden ray of hope shone through her depression. If her daughter cared enough to make offerings to her father, perhaps she would pay a call on her as well. Why couldn't she get on with her daughter as the peasant women did with theirs and live out her life in contentment? She almost called out, but she couldn't drop her defenses that far. Then it occurred to her that her daughter would have to pass right by her house on her way home, so she decided to go first and make her a special meal.

Back at home, she rolled up her sleeves and got busy. Time was tight—she couldn't go out and buy fresh ingredients or grind glutinous rice into flour for the traditional dumplings. Fortunately, she had a well-stocked larder—cans of luxury food not available to mere peasants: sausage, dried shredded meat, pressed chicken . . . she soon had a dozen plates of food and a bottle of red wine laid out on the table. In case that wasn't enough, she filled bowls with melon seeds and candies and even measured some malted milk powder into a glass, with hot water ready to add when her daughter arrived.

She would put on airs no longer. If her daughter would only come, she would give her anything; the dressing table of course, even a television. Her daughter might not agree to it all straight away, so perhaps she would start off with some new clothes for her granddaughter. Huang Huizhen resolved that she would not even oppose her daughter if she said she wanted another child; why, she would even make a contribution to help pay the fine. She had money, and what she would really like was a chubby little grandson making little messes on the floor and wetting the sheets. . . .

She waited until the dishes on the table were all cold, but still there was no sign of her daughter. Impatient, she went back to look for her. She rushed in a panic to the bamboo grove across the river from the graves. All she could see were the green grave mounds and the strings of paper cash fluttering like butterflies in the breeze. The pines, still without new growth, stood somber and dark, grief-stricken as a widow. There was nobody there. Her daughter was gone.

Huang Huizhen felt dizzy. The bamboo grove whirled around, the river flowing above her, dark yellow waves rushing toward her . . . the world was turning upside down. She groaned and grasped hold of a slim bamboo. But it wouldn't hold her up, and she slumped to the ground.

Beyond the shade of the bamboo grove, there was the red of peach blossoms and the green of willows. Shafts of sunset red as tulip petals caressed the fields. And in the fields, the golden rape, the snow-white magnolia, the pink flowers of the broad beans . . . however fierce the wind might be, however hard the rain, the earth would come to life, the flowers would bloom again.

Night Songs

—1—

At dusk, in the sporadic gusts of an aimless southern breeze, a two-stringed fiddle that had lain silent for thirty years scratched, grated, and came back to life. Blind Old Pots sat in his doorway, playing and singing:

> *"Pots sings to tell his tale,*
> *Pots plays for me.*
> *Add the master to us both,*
> *and people there are three. . ."*

These were the opening lines that began a thousand songs; back in the days when he had performed at the brigade's Hall of Culture, he had always started off this way. Some of the audience would chide him: "Does that mean we're not 'people'? Are you telling us that the 'master' in the temple, that crumbling old bodhisattva, is a 'person' and we're not?"

Still, nobody really took offense. The words the fiddle, the sad rasping voice, the black peasant jacket that he wore year round, all seemed to add to Pots' mystique. Old and feeble he might be, but he clung tenaciously to life, like a boulder submerged at high tide resurfacing when the waves recede, pitted and scarred, crevices filled with moss and waterweeds, but still unbroken, waiting out the years and months as waters rise and fall.

At sundown the previous day, a little skiff had drifted in on the willow-shrouded Slanting Brook. In the evening light the willow fronds were like patches of mist, bordered by the rose of sunset, the colors of fresh green scallions. The skiff moved on unhurriedly. White butterflies flitted in the undergrowth. Lentils bloomed by the roadside, but they were outdone by the redbuds that grew by the fences, stamens furry like the bodies of bees, setting off the mauve of their petals.

The stream was clear and shallow. Unprepared to take on itself the rich variety of colors on the bank, it merely draped a few strands of the sunset's red over its slender waist. Dark ripples glinted like the scales of a fish as the water flowed under the rickety bridge, sluggish as the movement of the darkening sky.

As the skiff came under the bridge, paddies stretched endless and vivid green before it, disappearing into the gray of the horizon. A water buffalo with high curving horns ambled along the dike between two fields, robust and massive, its black skin glossy as satin. The old man who led the buffalo was hunched like a withered eggplant in his blue jacket.

The music of the fiddle wafted intermittently on the chill breeze, its plaintive melody repeating songs of grief and accusation. As the boat headed toward the source of the music, the sound seemed to touch the two women on board.

The mooring was by the bridge at the head of the village. The two women alighted from the boat. The younger one was in her forties, a few strands of gray in her hair, strongly built, and still quite agile as she helped the other off the boat. This one was elderly, her face wrinkled like a walnut shell, her thin straggling hair too sparse to cover her scalp. The younger woman addressed her as "Ma." "Ma," she said, "it'll be fine here." The old one nodded. Then they went back on board to fetch a small grindstone, a shabby cloth bag, and a bedding roll. The old one still had some strength in her and helped with their few possessions.

A crowd of children gathered on the bank, along with some older passersby who had stopped to look. In years past they had seldom seen drifters like these two, but a recent change in government policy had allowed villagers to leave their homes to pursue "alternative enterprises." This had brought peddlers from Shandong selling preserved ginger from their barrows, quilt repairers from Anhui, and weavers of bamboo mats from Zhejiang. There were tinkers, riveters, cobblers, makers of puffed rice and bean curd . . . the onlookers surmised that this mother and daughter probably made their living selling bean curd, though such wretchedly poor people were seldom seen. Where had they come from, and where would they go from here? What did they have to live on? And where would they find lodging so late in the day?

Sympathetic though the onlookers might be, when the two women pleaded for someone to let them stay the night, nobody said a word. They hadn't always been so inhospitable. In years past anyone would have welcomed such travelers. But back then they had all lived in cottages or thatched huts; now they had proper two-story houses. Back then everyone had gone hungry; now their larders were well stocked, and there were televisions in every home. So naturally they couldn't do as their fathers would have done and allow perfect strangers to spend a night under their roofs.

One of them came up with an idea: "Hey, why don't you go stay with Blind Old Pots?"

Some bright spark chipped in, "Sure, he's got lots of room! And he's bound to be lonesome with all that space to himself. Go along there. You might cheer him up."

It wasn't really true about the space. Pots lived in the last two-room shack in the village, and how could that be as spacious as these people's big houses? It was right enough that Pots lived alone, though nobody had ever taken the trouble to ask him if he felt the need of company. The real reason for the suggestion was that Pots' only property was his old fiddle, which wouldn't interest these two women. All in all, suggesting that they seek shelter with Pots didn't seem like such a bad idea.

—2—

Through that long night, Blind Pots couldn't make up his mind whether he was asleep or awake. He felt that he was suffocating in his own grave, with no blood in his veins, no hair, no skin, all his senses gone with his sight. Nothing remained to him but a set of white bones. Yet somehow this skeleton was not dead; there was some spirit from the netherworld whose sole duty was to look after him, as if it were protecting some shard of broken pottery tossed aside by primitive man.

Late at night—or perhaps it was early morning—it seemed that a tiny crack opened in the dark stillness of his tomb, letting in a ray of light, pale and faint as a bean sprout.

In the next room mother and daughter were setting up their grindstone. The daughter yawned as she brought in the soaked beans. The mother said, "Fragrance, you take a rest, and let me do the grinding for you. Older people don't need as much sleep."

The daughter shook her head: "Ma, you can sleep if you're tired."

The older woman tried again: "Then sing a little song to keep us awake."

The daughter giggled: "What songs do I know? Only 'If You're Going to Wear a Flower, Wear a Red Flower' and 'With the Precious Book in My Hand My Heart Turns to the Party.' Or else the 'Howl of the Demons and Monsters' that they made me sing when I was being criticized."

"Silly girl, going on about that all over again!" The mother hastily interrupted her daughter, as if she feared such talk would bring them bad luck. "Ma will sing for you. I knew a lot of songs when I was young."

Laughing, the daughter encouraged her mother to sing, all weariness gone from her voice. The grindstone squeaked as it turned, red husks piling up as the white bean milk started to drip down.

The old woman sang softly:

"Push and pull, oh so hard,
The stone turns round like a wheel."

The voice was low and husky with age, yet its song, sad and plaintive, seemed to breathe new life into the shack. At that moment, Pots felt his tomb being torn asunder. A light shone, so powerful that he could not open his eyes, and the grindstone, the bean milk, and the lost years all burst forth from under the ground. A mighty force knocked him sprawling. He felt no pain, heaved himself to his feet, and felt around for his fiddle. Then, shaking from head to foot, he started to play like a man possessed.

The noise shocked the women in the next room. The daughter gasped in alarm, "Ma! We've woken Uncle with our grinding and singing, and this is how he protests."

Obediently, the mother stopped singing.

The fiddle shrieked on with furious abandon, playing the same tune that the old woman had been singing, repeating it over and over again, like a plea, like a call to arms, reaching into their hearts to pluck something out.

But the singing in the other room was silenced. Only the doleful creak of the grindstone accompanied the fiddle. Pots played on for a while, then sang himself the rest of the verse that the old bean-curd maker had begun:

"Thanks kind Uncle for your help,
You knew how I feel."

Thus he played and sang till dawn, to the consternation of the women. In the morning, the mother sent her daughter round to check on him and give him a bowl of hot bean milk. Fragrance saw the blind old man sitting on the ground, dirty and disheveled like a ghost. She asked him nothing, but sighed as she set the bowl beside him: "Have some bean milk, Uncle; it will calm you down."

At the sound of her voice, the old man's hand relaxed; the fiddle slipped from his grasp and fell to the ground. He did not reach for the bowl, just sat there in a daze. Nothing had happened, nothing at all. Today was like yesterdays without number, exactly the same. What is lost can never be recovered.

That river too had been long and narrow, soft and sinuous as it wound its way through open country and dense foliage. There, too, spring breezes blew along banks shrouded by willows, the clouds of dusk lit the sky with rich colors, and the wind sighed in the trees. But that was not Slanting Brook. It was called . . . yes, it was Cat's Ear, Cat's Ear Stream, an odd name for a river, but not unpleasant.

Every day he would pilot his little boat up and down the river, careless and free-spirited as a fish.

He had no land along the bank and no family. Yet he didn't feel the slightest regret. He had Cat's Ear Stream. There were fish and shrimp in the river, and that was enough to occupy him without melancholy or concern.

He made up his mind not to fish anywhere else. He set his pots down in large numbers at the bend in the river.

There was a girl who came to the bridge with a pair of wooden buckets, to draw water from the river. She wore a thin jacket, so tattered that even the patches were patched, and her feet were frozen raw in their straw sandals. The girl's only adornment was a thick braid, which hung straight down to her waist or else slipped forward and curled enchantingly across her breast. He watched her in awe and decided that this would be just the spot to set his shrimp pots.

When her wooden buckets were full, they were as heavy as mountains, weighing down the girl's slender frame. It pained him to watch her carrying them—he felt that she shouldn't have to bear such a heavy load. So he jumped onto the bank and picked up her carrying pole. On his powerful shoulder, the huge buckets were as light as bundles of rushes. His shoulders were strong and steady and his chest broad.

They followed a little path through a shady bamboo grove until he saw a trellis of beans standing by a grindstone, with a two-room thatched cottage behind. He carried the water to this point and then set the buckets down. He wouldn't go beyond the bamboo grove. Under cover of the bamboos he watched as she struggled down to the grindstone with a load that must have been twice her own weight.

In the cottage behind the grindstone lived an old woman made mean and cantankerous by poverty and the woman's moronic son. She had been widowed young, and her son was seven years old before he spoke a word. The woman was so unpleasant that the other members of the clan all hoped that her branch of the family would die out. None of them invited her to weddings, funerals, or the feasts held to celebrate babies surviving their first month. All avoided her for fear that her ill fortune might rub off on them. Still, one morning her luck took a turn for the better. She was out cutting grass when she came across a baby at the roadside, wrapped in a bundle and yelling for all she was worth. The woman walked past her but could still hear her clearly from well down the road. She thought for a moment of all the hateful things her neighbors were saying about her, and then, quite suddenly, she had an idea. She turned back, put the baby in her basket, and took her home. Needing a baby name for the child, she called her Bunny, since she found her when she was out cutting grass to feed her rabbits.

Of course, the woman wasn't raising the girl out of the goodness of her heart. By the time she was six, Bunny was expected to do the cooking, and at nine she was set to work turning the grindstone. She wasn't allowed to eat at the table or given a bed to sleep in at night. And, once the girl reached puberty, the old woman expected her to marry her son.

When Pots learned of the fate that awaited the girl, he tossed and turned all night in his little cabin by the riverbank. Like him, she had neither father nor mother; life had treated them both bitterly. The bitterness of their lives was a force that would bind them together. The plaster of paris used in making bean curd is bitter, but it makes the bean milk coagulate, and life's bitterness could bind their two hearts together in the same way.

He became bolder. On days when he knew for certain that the old woman was not at home, he would carry the water out of the bamboo grove, right up to the trellis. When the old woman was away selling bean curd, he would go over and help the girl at the grindstone. The old woman had to travel long distances to sell her bean curd since nobody nearby would buy it. They detested her swarthy face, which even in youth had been pitted and scarred, and the red and yellow pus that oozed from the corners of her eyes.

As Pots turned the grindstone with the girl, he felt a new and gloriously sweet sensation. The sky was so blue, the river water so pure, the birdsong so vivid, that something welling up inside him forced him to burst forth in song; and the only song that came to mind was the one that the young widow sings in the opera *Two at the Grindstone:*

"Pushing, pulling, life's so hard,
The stone turns round like a wheel."

Pots was an intelligent lad. He'd only seen the opera once, sneaking in through the crowd one day when he happened to be in town selling shrimps. He hadn't had a seat, instead squatting down to watch, and by the time he came away he could sing the opera just the way the actors had performed it.

It turned out that the girl had a good ear, too. After she had heard Pots sing a couple of times, she smiled impishly and took up the song:

"Thanks kind Uncle for your help,
You knew how I feel."

Her voice was light and sweet as milk, with no trace of sadness. Pots' whole body went soft, as if he were drunk. He took his hands off the grindstone and stared at the girl, his eyes burning with first love.

She asked him: "What's wrong, Brother Pots?"

"I want you for my wife," he answered.

The girl trembled and leaned weakly against the grindstone. Pots went over to her to hold her, but she pushed him away and said in alarm, "Brother Pots, you mustn't ever say such a thing again. Don't . . . don't come back here anymore. You have to be careful . . . don't let Mama see you. She's evil, she can hit and pinch. . . . Really, I'm not fooling you. You must be careful."

Without a word, Pots took the girl's delicate hand, then gently pushed her sleeve up from her wrist. The arm was thin as a child's and covered with angry black and purple welts. His eyelids trembled, and two hot tears fell onto the girl's bruised arms.

"You can't really want to marry that moron and look after him the rest of your life?" Pots demanded.

The child bride shook her head and said she didn't know.

Pots put his mouth to her ear and whispered, "These days in the cities they say you can . . . pick freely."

The words meant nothing to the girl: "What do you mean . . . pig's belly?"

"No, I said 'pick freely': that means being allowed to do what you want to." Pots explained as best he could.

She giggled: "People aren't like dogs and cats; of course we can do what we want to. What's so strange about that?"

"Well," Pots asked her again, "do you really want to marry that moron?"

The smile vanished from the girl's face, replaced by a look of panic. She bit her lip and said nothing.

"What 'pick freely' really means is that men and women can love whoever they want to."

She blushed charmingly: "Do you mean it?" Without waiting for an answer, she continued, "Brother Pots, you're marvelous!"

Pots felt proud of himself and couldn't resist showing off a little: "When I've got some money together, I'll take you to see opera. We can stretch out in leather chairs and take it easy. Opera's got everything, it's . . . like . . . culture."

The girl could scarcely believe the joys that awaited her. Her heart was like a stream in spring, warm winds wafting across its surface.

The old woman became aware of the change in the girl she had raised. There was color in her cheeks, she looked prettier, she brushed her hair every day till it shone, and her clothing was neatly patched and mended. One day when the old woman was watching the child bride, she noticed that the scrap of cloth that the girl used to fasten her braid had been replaced by a piece of red woolen yarn and that she was wearing a new hairpin in the shape of a butterfly. Her suspicions aroused, the old woman angrily summoned the girl for questioning.

By the time the girl made her appearance, the hairpin had vanished, but there had been no time to change the red yarn, and there was the scent of sandalwood lingering on that glossy pigtail.

The old woman grabbed at the pigtail and jerked it hard: "Little bitch! How much of my money did you steal? Tell me, now!"

Cry out from the pain as she must, the girl did not say a word. Unable to get any answers from her, the old woman launched an intensive search. She examined the floor, turned over the haystack, and peered into the cracks in the masonry. Finally she discovered a bottle of sandalwood oil, a small mirror, a peachwood comb, and even a pair of stockings, the like of which she had herself never worn. Try as she might, she couldn't find a penny of her money missing, and she was at a loss to know where these things had come from. But from that moment on she was on her guard, her nose wrinkling to sniff out the answer. Finally she smelled it out: it must be that young fellow who came by to set his shrimp pots He was the one that threatened her son and herself! Now she would stand at the door and scream at Pots every time he brought his boat down Cat's Ear Stream, "There's that wild dog, come prowling round for a whiff of something tasty."

But Pots kept coming anyway. Why shouldn't he? He'd been to the opera, and he knew all about "pick freely" and "culture."

The old woman realized that screaming at him wasn't going to do the trick, so she went down to the stream and smashed his shrimp pots. Next day when Pots came by to check them and found them wrecked, he was livid. He straightened his neck and yelled right back at her, "Slut! Poisonous bitch!"

That was no way for a young man to be talking to her! The old woman took serious offense. Not knowing what she could do to get revenge, she went to see the clan head

The clan head was a village elder who was also the district chief. That job was retitled village head after Liberation and later still brigade chairman, though by then it was occupied by his son.

The old woman went to see the clan head, not so much because she had faith in him, but because it was the natural thing to do, like eating when hungry or drinking when thirsty. In fact the clan head had never shown any sympathy for her at all. The year her husband died, her son was dangerously ill. She had gone and kowtowed to the clan head, beating her head black and blue on the ground in front of his stinking shoes, and pleaded with him to lend her the fifty cents she needed to get a doctor for the baby. He figured that if he lent her the money, that would be the last he saw of it, so he offered her words of wisdom instead: "Doctors may treat sickness, but they can't cure destiny. A man's life span is ordained by heaven; if he's fated to live, he'll get better whether he sees a doctor or not; if he's fated to die young, no medicine can cure him. No sense wasting the money."

As it turned out, her son must have been fated to live. He did survive, but the illness left him weak in the head. Some people said that it was the clan head's callousness that was to blame for the boy's backwardness. Maybe that thought had never occurred to her, or maybe she'd forgotten the whole incident; anyway, she went back to the clan head and respectfully recounted her tale of woe.

He listened to her spluttering recital, puffing away at his water pipe.

Suddenly aware of how insignificant and contemptible she must seem, the old woman was near panic. Her legs felt weak, and she was on the verge of collapsing to her knees when he finally spoke: "Is the girl fourteen yet?"

"More, Sir. She'll be sixteen this fall."

The clan head grunted. "Girl that age should be married."

These were the words of a sage! The woman bowed her head and cursed herself for being so stupid. Of course! If she could get the marriage over and done with as soon as possible, then that would be the end of her problems.

But when she got home and gave the matter some thought, she realized it wasn't quite as simple as all that. It wasn't that she hadn't considered marrying them, just that weddings cost money. Her son might be backward, but he was her only child and the sole hope for keeping the family line going. Her original plan had been to wait until winter and have the wedding when she'd sold the pig; now she felt that that was too long to wait. After all, the pig wasn't some lump of bubble gum that would swell up on demand. After some thought, she summoned the boy before her and issued a command: "You're not staying with Mummy tonight. Go and sleep with that little tramp in the other room—she's your lady now, understand?"

The moron was delighted and hurried in as soon as it was dark. The girl's bed was in a storeroom next to where the old lady slept. The door wasn't bolted. The girl hadn't gone to sleep but was sprawled on a pile of rice stalks lost in sweet thoughts of her Brother Pots. When the moron burst in and tried to cuddle up to her, she dodged out of his way: "What's up with you!"

He giggled: "Mummy says I got to go to bed with you."

The girl shook with fury. "Out! Out!" she ordered, shoving at him, but she couldn't get him to move. Frustrated, she boxed his ears. He was stunned for a moment, then shuffled out with his head in his hands.

His mother scolded him: "Useless brute! Idiot! Why'd you have to be in such a rush? Go in the night, when she's asleep, and be quiet about it, get it?"

He nodded, but she still wasn't sure he understood, so she spelled it out for him: "When you go in, take off her clothes first, and then undress yourself."

"Won't that be cold, Mummy?" the boy whimpered.

"You won't be cold."

The next night the girl lay awake, not daring to close her eyes in case he burst in on her again. It wasn't until the early hours of the morning that she finally sank into a troubled sleep. Then the moron came again, softly this time so as not to wake her up. He crept to her bed, drew back the covers, and pulled off her clothes. As her white body appeared before his eyes, he trembled, the blood boiling inside him. Mummy was right; he didn't feel cold, not even a bit. So he did exactly as she had told him and stripped himself naked.

The girl woke from a nightmare to see the moron standing there like a savage. She screamed in terror, as if she'd seen a demon. But in the vastness of that black night her screams were as insignificant as a grain of dust, unnoticed by all. The moron sprang on her, like someone famished and parched who comes on a juicy slice of lotus root and wants to gobble it all up in one gulp.

The girl realized that it was the old woman who had put him up to this, so there wasn't any point calling to her for help. Nobody could save her but herself. So she stopped yelling and fought back with all her strength, scratching and biting till his face and body were torn and bleeding. He might be the stronger, but he was slow and clumsy. Finally he slunk away to nurse his wounds.

In the adjoining room, the old woman listened anxiously and angrily. She had never imagined that the girl would put up such resistance, and it infuriated her. She told her son, "Tie her hands and feet next time, and we'll see if she's still as stubborn."

The following night, the moon shone yellow, and the wind was soft. Alone and helpless, the child bride was raped by the moron. Without a word, the girl dressed in her best, walked out of the house and through the bamboo grove, and took the path along Cat's Ear Stream for several miles until she found the one-room cabin where Pots lived.

"Brother Pots, please take me."

Pots was overjoyed: "What? You want to 'pick freely'?"

The girl was silent, her eyes tight shut, tears of anguish running down her face.

And so Pots took her in. His little boat bobbed empty in the stream outside the cabin, as a gentle dew descended on the fields in the misty night. Pots said, "We'll go far away from here, and the old woman and the moron will never see you again."

When she found the child bride gone, the old woman screamed and wailed. She kowtowed to the clan head, bruising her head on his stinking shoes: "Take pity on a poor widow and her only son! We worked so hard to raise that child bride, and now the little bitch has run off with some good-for-nothing! I appeal for your protection!"

On this occasion the clan head was uncharacteristically considerate, helping her to her feet without even waiting for her head to start bleeding: "Come now, Aunty, no need for that from you; you're the older generation after all. The child bride's actions are in violation of custom and propriety. Leave this to me!"

The old woman was still choking: "But she's run away, and I don't know where she's gone!"

The clan head's voice was cold and stern: "Don't worry! They can run to the ends of the earth if they want. We'll catch them!"

The old woman was as grateful as if he'd saved her life. But the clan head's daughter, a girl about the same age as the child bride, whispered, "Shame to hunt for such a pretty girl just to make her marry an idiot."

Her voice was soft, but her father heard it clearly enough. "Where's the shame in it? She's a woman, so she's a cheap life, and she can do as she's told. Marry her to a rooster or a dog, and that's what she gets!"

The daughter wasn't giving up so easily. "Aren't women people too?" she hissed. "Are Granny and Mummy just chickens or dogs?"

Her father was steaming mad. He pounded on the table: "Shut your damn mouth!" he roared.

The clan head's wife hurried over to pull her away, scolding her as they went: "Silly girl, don't you understand? If you raise a buffalo, you use it to pull a plow; if you raise a pig or chicken, you slaughter it for food; and if you raise a child bride, you keep her to be a daughter-in-law and carry on the family line. That's right and proper, and her being pretty is neither here nor there. If they hadn't picked her up when she was a baby, she'd have died right away, and being pretty wouldn't have made any difference then. What right's she got to refuse him just because he's a moron?"

The girl was still unrepentant and grumbling. So the clan head laid down the law, his eyes bulging with rage: "Listen to your mother! Women are worth no more than chickens and dogs! That's always been the rule, and don't let anyone dare break it!"

The clan head withdrew to plan his next move. He summoned other clan elders to his place for nights on end, where they drank gallons of tea and smoked several pounds of tobacco. For once they were in agreement, united in their righteous indignation. None of them allowed their distaste for the old woman to hold them back; differences between them were overcome by their desire for revenge on a common enemy. They vowed that they would hunt the girl down and bring her back.

But Pots proved to be a cunning quarry. His little love boat moved softly as a mirage, bobbing up where it was least expected, coming without a shadow and leaving without a trace.

Every now and then there would be a report: "Someone saw Pots selling shrimp in town," or "Pots was seen fishing in Gongsun Creek to the west of Cat's Ear Stream."

But every time the posse followed him, they came back empty-handed.

Summer turned to fall. The leaves thinned, and the river became colder, and still Pots hadn't been caught.

The old woman was frantic. Every day she went to the clan head to kowtow. His voice was menacing: "It will be winter soon, and they won't be able to live on the boat. They'll come ashore to sleep in his cabin, and when they do, we'll have them!"

One evening in the winter of 1947, as the first snows were falling on the Jiangnan plain, a group of several dozen men armed with carrying poles and pitchforks surrounded the little cabin on the banks of the Cat's Ear Stream. The two young lovers inside were seized without a struggle and tied up. It had all gone so smoothly that the band of bravos felt a bit let down. They had been expecting that ruffians would come pouring out of the woods to defend Pots and were ready for a good fight, but nothing of the sort had taken place.

Everything was snowbound and silent. A couple of dogs barked briefly in neighboring houses and then fell silent. The victors were quite pleased with themselves, and in the circumstances they didn't feel the need to beat Pots to death. Of course they couldn't just let him go, in case he came back and made more trouble for them later on. So after they had knocked him around a bit, they took out some quicklime that they had brought with them and rubbed it into his eyes.

Pots screamed and writhed in agony on the ground, carving a muddy trail through the snow as he clawed his way down toward the river. The sky, the ground, the river, and the willows, everything that had ever been between heaven and earth, all disappeared forever as Pots crawled into a white fog of despair.

And from the far side of the bank, which Pots would never see again, came the last cry of the child bride: "Brother Pots, wait for me! I'll come back! I'll find you!"

Pots crawled on. . . .

—3—

Throughout the long day, the blind old man sat in his doorway sunning himself. The rice was turning to gold in the fields, stalks stiff and brittle, leaves drying out and shining translucent in the sunlight. It was almost time to bring out the sickles and set to work harvesting. Everyone was busy; only the blind man had nothing to do.

The sun was hot, and the air was fragrant with hay. Every now and then a breeze would blow by, flicking yellow leaves that fluttered like butterflies around his face. They stuck to his head and fell down on his shoulders, but he seemed unconcerned with them. Another gust of wind would blow them away again. These withered leaves, tossed down from the branches of life, seemed to bear a heavy burden and whimpered softly in their swirling flight. The fiddle lay silent in his hand, as if he could not think of a song to play.

He sat uneasily, looking into his own eternal darkness on this radiant day.

Suddenly, a snatch of coquettish song echoed over the fields—

"Little sister sings, and her young man plays,
You and I are one heart always . . ."

—in waves of sound powerful enough to blow back a corner of the curtain of his darkness and let in a ray of light. This voice and its melody excited him; it wasn't *Two at the Grindstone,* so why did it seem so familiar? When had the sound of a song on the public address system ever sounded so sweet? He remembered how, for years and years, the loudspeakers rigged up near the fields had played nothing but heroic songs and fine-sounding slogans.

Try as he might, he could make no sense of it all; perhaps that was just the way life was.

"Candy! Candy! Trade for candy!" The old peddler beat on his hand drum and chanted as he came into the village to trade candies for waste. Snotty-nosed children would hear him coming and run for their homes, then hurry out again clasping household refuse—empty bottles, scraps of paper, rags of clothes, and frayed ropes. Then came the jeering of older bullies, and the wailing of smaller children who had been knocked to the ground, and the whining of children who felt that they hadn't been given as much candy as they deserved. And when all those voices were silent, the cry of the peddler would be heard again: "Candy! Candy! Trade for candy!" Barter of one thing for another, with no money involved, had been going on from time immemorial. In the blind man's hazy memories of his childhood, he recalled traders like this one, each with his hand drum. He had been greedy for candy, too, trading a string of little fish for ten candies and getting a thrashing from his father that left his buttocks red and sore.

A mother hen pecked at the blind man's foot, but he did not pull back. Instead it was the hen that decided that the foot was not to her taste, and she went clucking off in search of food.

It must be the beginning of the day, since he'd only just heard the call of the rabbit-fur buyer from the main road into the village. This young fellow would come by three times a day, his calls as precisely timed as the broadcasts over the public address. From now to noon, and then to dusk, more would follow—the mat weaver, the basket maker, and the sellers of bamboo steamers and wicker coils. Their calls echoed constantly around the village, high and low, coarse and refined. It was strange the way these people seemed to have come out of nowhere. How had trades that had been proscribed for so many years been relearned so quickly? Take the wicker coils called "snakes," which were woven out of strips shaved from bamboo. In days gone by people would coil them around and around to make storage bins for rice. Every household in the Jiangnan region would have one of these bins, and the craft of making them had been handed down from generation to generation of artisans. Nobody knew when these snake coils had first been made; people must have come up with this method of storing grain at the same time as they had learned how to grow it. But thirty years before, at the time of collectivization, the brigade had built an imposing concrete granary, and the old way of storing grain had fallen into disuse. As the saying went, "When the river has water, the streams are full"—the grain was stored by the collective, and anyone who wanted any could just go along with a bag and weigh some out, so who needed snake coils any longer?

Now the land had been divided again, and people were farming for themselves. The brigade granary was closed and empty, and every family had a full grain bin. Sellers of the snake coils were showing up all over the place, and said to be making a good living. Some of them were among the newly rich "ten-thousand-yuan households" being celebrated in the press. As the times changed, it was hard to know whether the world was going forward or backward.

Slanting Brook ran past the door, circled around an island shaped like a lotus leaf, and flowed on again. In both directions it was the same stream, with the same bridges, and much the same scenery. The blind man had never seen the stream, but he had felt his way along its banks countless times, and in his imagination Slanting Brook and Cat's Ear Stream were one and the same. In fact, this whole region was crisscrossed with waterways, and all the rivers and streams were pretty much the same, long and thin, with willows and reeds on their banks and waterweed on their surface, meandering around eyots and peninsulas and cutting through villages and bamboo groves.

The locals complained endlessly about the rivers: "They used to be so clear, you could see waterweed growing on the bottom, and watch shrimp and fish swimming about. But now the water is all murky with chemical waste from the factories; sometimes it's black, sometimes it's green, and sometimes it stinks." Others had different complaints: "The river's polluted, the fish taste of sulphur, and eating them gives you cancer."

Well, clear or murky, the blind man couldn't see it anyway, and it wouldn't bother him if he got cancer. As the saying goes, "Sixty-six, sixes doubling, bean curd boiling hot and bubbling"—the funeral feast is waiting, and death can't be far away. At that stage, the past is a mist, and what is there ahead to live for? Love and hate, sweet and sour, hot and bitter, all these sensations are reserved for the young. But the grief of separation was something he felt desperately. Sometimes as he set out with his beggar's staff, he would hear wild rabbits scurrying around his feet. Then his heart would pound, and he would stop and listen for hours, wondering if those could be the footsteps of his own little Bunny. When he heard girls' voices, chattering, laughing, or crying, he would listen intently to hear what they were saying. Someone had told him that after Bunny had been taken from him, she had run away again, back to where his boat had been, and at this news he had started to walk along the waterways. The network of streams was like a maze, but he had walked them all, with only his bamboo staff to help him find his way. At the first sound, be it the creak of an oar, the throaty cries of the cormorant fishermen calling in their birds, or the plashing of nets being hauled in against the boats, he would come to a halt and sing his *Two at the Grindstone* song over and over. He couldn't see Bunny, but she would see him, or she would hear his singing and follow the sound to him. Spring came, and the willows by the river came into bud, their soft catkins brushing against his face and forehead. As he sang, he thought that Bunny would see the willows come to life and think of the joyful time that they had spent together. And then, when winter came and snow filled the air and piled on his head, he would still stand and sing. Bunny will see the snow, he thought. She'll remember the moment we were parted.

Later on he stopped singing his *Two at the Grindstone* song. Instead he composed a new song about how he and Bunny had loved and been torn from each other. He felt that even if she didn't hear the song herself, the fishermen who heard might pass the story on to her, and then she would come and find him. . . .

From that time forth, through the years of separation, summer and winter, day in, day out, beneath the setting sun, wherever the fishermen moored their boats, there would be the sound of Pots' song. His voice was hoarse, he spat blood, but still he sang. To the world he was insane; only he knew what he felt and what he sought.

He had broken many staffs, but still he had not found Bunny. More and more people came to the conclusion that he was crazy, so they locked him away in a derelict temple. This was a strange place, known as Piss Temple and used as an asylum. The madmen and madwomen were all kept chained before the shrine, ostensibly so that they could be cured by the bodhisattva. Pots was big and strong, so they kept him shackled to a millstone. By the time he finally got away from Piss Temple he felt that he'd already died and been through hell. He gave up both his search and his singing. He was dead wood, and he stayed on in that small village, utterly dependent on the charity of the community.

The other pensioners in the brigade were elderly widows, all of whom had relatives somewhere and small tile-roofed cottages to live in. The younger generation among the distant relatives would have designs on their cottages, and so would come over at New Year and other holidays bearing festive delicacies. Pots had no relatives at all and lived in an old storage shed that belonged to the brigade. The shed was large enough, but it was drafty, and the windows were high and small. In winter he would find someone to stuff the window openings with rice straw, and in summer he would pull the straw back out again. In all the years that he had been there, he could only remember his quilt being washed three times. The first time had been during a campaign to learn from Chairman Mao's good soldier Lei Feng, and a swarm of children from the local elementary school had been on the lookout for good deeds to perform. They hadn't just washed his quilt—they'd also drawn water to fill his water vat and cooked him a meal of sweet-smelling rice. To this day he still had fond memories of those children. They had been the only warmth in the monotony of his life. The second time was when the government sent an official down to the lower levels and billeted him with Pots. Either as a result of the ideological transformation of the official class, or because he was afraid lice might jump from Pots' bed onto him, the official screwed up his nose and washed the quilt, which by then was the same color as the planks on which it rested. The third time was just a couple of days ago, when the mother and daughter bean-curd makers had come into his dark room, swept away the dust and the spiders' webs, and taken out the shabby quilt, handling it gently for fear that it would fall to pieces.

Cleaning it must have been quite a task for them. He overheard the daughter asking, "Ma, are we going to be able to sew it up when we've washed it?"

The mother said, "See if we've got any decent-sized pieces of cloth in our stuff to patch it with."

Finally the quilt was clean and neatly mended. As it rested softly on his skin, it gave off a fragrance from being dried and aired in the sun that was like a woman's sweet breath.

In all his life, the blind man had never paid attention to any woman but Bunny. When these two women came to him, he had neither nodded nor shaken his head at their request to stay with him, his face cold and expressionless in tacit consent. Later on, when they had tried to talk to him, he had merely grunted, as if he were dumb as well as blind. But still the two women had done their utmost to care for him. When they left the hut in the morning, they would leave two cakes of bean curd, and in the evening they would prepare a hot meal and invite him in to eat with them. If he had been able to open his eyes, he would have seen how spotless the room had become. He did notice that the musty smell that he had lived with for years was gone, replaced by the mild clean scent of bean curd, the smell of cheap soap, and the aroma of cooking. Added to that was the soft tread of footsteps, the rustle of a broom on the dirt floor, and the tinkle of chopsticks on pots and bowls —all of which combined in a warm spring of femininity, whose gentle waters washed and revived the stone heart of Old Pots. In his wilder moments, he even allowed himself to imagine that the older of these two women might possibly be his girl, Bunny. She couldn't really be, of course. If she had been Bunny, she'd have recognized him long ago. He might be blind and unable to see her, but she could still see him! Even if he was unrecognizable as his former self, she had heard his song, and she would have responded! What reason could she have for not doing so? But what if his voice had changed so much that she could not recognize it? This wasn't out of the question. And if his voice could have changed so much, then what about hers? Would he even know Bunny's voice after all these years? Strangely enough, there had been times when mother and daughter had got up in the middle of the night to grind their beans, their voices low to avoid disturbing him, and he had been convinced that Bunny was before him. But she hadn't changed at all; she was just as she had been back then at that other grindstone.

One day, with pretended casualness, he had asked their ages, and their answers had shocked him greatly. It turned out that the mother was exactly Bunny's age and the daughter was forty-two. He fantasized that she could even be his own daughter—Bunny had been with child when she was dragged away from him.

Such wild imaginings seemed absurd even to him; but they nagged away at him, and he couldn't set them aside. Every day he sat at his door, waiting for the footsteps of the women returning from their bean-curd selling, deluding himself that they were Bunny and his daughter. Time and again he had readied himself to ask them about their past, but had been afraid that by doing so he might destroy the dream he cherished so dearly. The longer this went on, the more rich and colorful his fantasy became, and the more recklessly he embroidered details into the tapestry of his longings.

One day the women measured his feet. They told him that

with the cold weather coming on, they should make him a pair of cotton-padded shoes. His heart flushed, and he suddenly remembered that Bunny had once measured his feet in the same way, just before winter came, and then sat up all night to make him a pair of padded shoes.

He could bear the suspense no longer. He made up his mind that he would question the mother and daughter and find out the truth.

—4—

The bean-curd seller pitied the blind man's sufferings, but she really wasn't Bunny. Nor had she ever been a child bride. Her family had been poor, but they had still pampered her. Her father had named her Chrysanthemum because she had been born in the ninth month. The year she turned fifteen, she was married with what was, for those days, quite a respectable dowry.

After some years of marriage, she remained childless. This was a source of great aggravation to her husband who drank heavily to relieve his frustration. After one bout of drinking, he took out his little boat to cast nets in the shallows. In a momentary lapse, he overturned the boat and tumbled into the water. She was carrying mud from the bank when it happened; dizzy from shock, she still managed to cry out for help. As luck would have it, there was a convoy making its way upstream, the boats a fine sight with their awnings of woven reeds. The oarsmen were stripped to the waist, revealing powerful torsos and brawny arms burned to the color of mahogany, muscular and virile. She yelled to them, "Help, please! Uncles, save him!"

Her husband was thrashing wildly about in the river, his hair surfacing and then submerging again, but the men on the boats acted as if they had seen nothing, not even raising their eyes, indifferent and proud. In a panic, she knelt down on the bank and kowtowed toward the line of barges, as her heart-rending cries drove the birds from the trees. At last the hairy-chested man on the prow of the leading boat turned his gaze on her and frowned—or perhaps it wasn't a frown since his eyebrows were joined together to start with. Then, in a gesture of annoyance and impatience, he spat, and the gob of spittle landed on the tuft of hair floating in the river, the hair of the drowning man. The others squatting on deck began to laugh, either at her kowtowing or at some private joke of their own. The convoy of boats kept on going, and a snatch of lewd song drifted back to her:

"Hands a-groping bit by bit
For a squeeze of Sister's tit,
How's her tits feel in your hand?
Like fresh-baked dumplings on the stand!"

In her despair, she paid no heed to their malice. Forgetting that she couldn't swim, she plunged into the water. But she failed to save her husband and gulped in a bellyful of water before losing consciousness herself.

When she came to, she discovered that she was lying cradled in the arms of a young woman. The woman was beautiful, but her face was ashen. Jet-black hair fell loosely over her shoulders, and her whole body was soaking wet.

Realizing that the woman had saved her life, she rolled over onto the ground and kowtowed to thank this elder sister for her kindness. But the woman only turned away and started to cry softly. She cried too, cried for her drowned man. What it was the other was crying for she did not know.

They cried for a long time. The next time she looked up, the sun was setting, lighting the surface of the river to the color of blood. Smoke was curling up out of the blood glow as food was cooked on the convoy of boats now moored downriver.

They bowed their heads and wept again. The sun had completely set, and, in the chill and forlorn evening air, a waning crescent moon rose up. On the silent river, the lights of the fishing boats twinkled like fireflies, as their occupants caught fish and crabs or set their shrimp pot.

The next day the convoy of boats had gone, but the sister was still there, and she had with her a three-year-old girl.

Actually the men on the boats weren't really fishermen at all. They were more like a pack of thieves or vagabonds. They made their home on the boats, sometimes doing a little fishing, sometimes heading ashore to beg, pilfer, or plunder. Frequently a horde of these vagabonds, male and female, would descend on a village. If they saw rice, New Year's cake, or beans left to dry outside the houses, they would stuff them into their packs and swagger away; they plucked fresh corncobs in the fields and picked fruit and vegetables from the gardens; they pulled down the salted fish and cured meats that the peasants had hung from the eaves and grabbed ducks and chickens from their pens. If the villagers came out to remonstrate with them, they attacked them with clubs; or if the villagers were better armed, the vagabonds would make a run for it. In the blinking of an eye, that convoy of ten boats would be gone, leaving the village stripped clean, without so much as a diaper left behind.

The people living on the banks were helpless before these lawless vagabonds. Whoever defied them risked having his house burned down in the middle of the night. Or else they might kidnap a child, and the next thing anyone knew there would be a ransom note delivered, demanding a large sum of money.

Even two years after Liberation, these boat dwellers had no household registration. They formed into bands around some kind of religious belief, with a leader known as the "Priest." The Priest would always have a pretty girl on hand, who would sleep with him when they were on the boat. When they went on shore, the girl would go off and seduce some man; then the Priest and his men would seize the unfortunate "adulterer" and extort a tidy sum of money from him.

It was part of the code of the vagabonds that shore dwellers who fell into the river were not to be saved. Anyone who rescued a drowning person had transgressed the "law of heaven." By saving Chrysanthemum, this young woman had broken the "law of heaven" and been thrown off the boat.

From this point on, these two wretched and friendless young women lived together. Chrysanthemum had been widowed young, so it was only to be expected that she would be melancholy, but the one who had saved her life was more mournful still. When Chrysanthemum was tired, she would cry for a while, then dry her tears and tell her new sister stories of things that had happened while her husband was alive. She would talk about her loving parents, how they done their best to find her a good family to marry into so that in death they could close their eyes in peace; never had they suspected that their daughter would be so tragically abandoned. After she had cried and talked, her pain would be eased. But Sister never said a word about her past life, never shed a tear, even as her dark eyes glistened with grief. Their only happiness was that little girl, who always seemed to want to nurse and chuckled contentedly when she was full.

It wasn't easy for the two women to keep body and soul together. Sister saw that Chrysanthemum had some soybeans in her house and suggested that they make them into bean curd and sell it. Sister was a skilled worker and could put up with hardship. She would get up in the middle of the night to turn the grindstone and make trips down to the river to draw water. Chrysanthemum became her assistant. Their bean curd was soft and white, and business was good. Whenever they made some money, Sister would buy candy or cake for her daughter. Once she bought a few feet of red cloth to make a cape to dress the girl up a little. But Sister's frown never eased;

she was always preoccupied. Sometimes when she went down to the river for water, she would gaze out at the returning fishing boats and stand in a daze, not even noticing when her wooden buckets started to float away. Late one night they heard a plaintive song from somewhere out on the river. Sister suddenly sat up, then scurried away, light as a cat. Chrysanthemum was terribly alarmed. Worried about what might happen, she dressed and followed stealthily after.

Sister ran all the way to the bank and stopped.

In the dark fastness of the lake was a single shabby fishing boat, an old man letting down his shrimp pots by the flickering light of his fishing lamps.

The pale moon lit Sister's pallid face. The willows trembled in the night air, and Sister's body shook too, as if she herself might be blown into the river like a withered blossom.

Chrysanthemum went over and held her: "Sister, Sister, it's all my fault. If it hadn't been for me, you'd be able to go back to the boats. I will go and kowtow to the Priest next time he's here. Then we'll offer him a gift so that he'll take you back."

Sister sighed and shook her head: "No, I wouldn't go back. It's no place for a person to be."

Chrysanthemum was amazed. If this were the case, what sadness was it that Sister was hiding from her?

After much thought, she decided that Sister must be lying. If she didn't want to go back to the boats, then why should the thought of a boat make her so distraught? It must be something to do with the boats that caused her such distress. So despite her hatred for the vagabonds, Chrysanthemum felt a secret longing for the convoy.

In no time it was New Year, and the wind blew cold off the water. All the leaves had fallen from the willows and the brush, leaving bare branches to reach up to heaven. There were no boats moored on the river, and no fishermen came by to set down shrimp pots.

But then one night the convoy of boats with reed awnings

came back without warning. They did not enter the village, instead mooring quietly outside. So dark was it that the boats went unnoticed by all but Chrysanthemum, who saw them on her way home from selling bean curd. Softly she told Sister, "They're back."

Sister didn't seem at all pleased with the news. Chrysanthemum said, "We won't sell bean curd tomorrow; we'll go and find the Priest."

Sister wouldn't hear of this, and the next day they sold bean curd as usual.

That day was the third of the New Year by the farmer's calendar, an auspicious day, and one of the village families was having a wedding. Firecrackers could be heard popping from early in the morning. Kettles for tea were bubbling fiercely, providing a constant supply of hot water. The people minding the kettles worked busily to provide hot towels; relatives and guests solemnly took their places in the main room of the house, which was decorated with paper lanterns and decked with brocade, as reed pipes and strings played to welcome them. In front of the hall the family had put up a shed, the kind used on special occasions for banquets.

People weren't as prosperous in those days. Even those families who were comfortably off would have only two- or three-room cottages, not big enough for a large gathering, so they had to put up a temporary shed for a big event. The host busied himself, and by noon the guests were all there, and everyone could be invited to eat. Of course the guests could not all take their places at the same time. As etiquette and deference required, the venerable and the important were seated first. But right at that moment, with a whoosh like a tornado, dozens of raggedly dressed men and women descended on the banquet. Someone groaned, "Oh no! It's the vagabonds!" Hardly had the words been spoken than the rabble shoved its way into the shed, taking all the seats at the table and pushing aside the people who were in the process of persuading each other to go in first.

The hot dishes had not yet been served, but cold platters and wine were already set out on the tables. The vagabonds gulped down the wine and grabbed handfuls of smoked fish, salted meat, cold sausages, and hacked chicken from the plates.

The guests looked helplessly at each other. The host was even more anxious and afraid, his legs trembling uncontrollably. He was aware of the rules of vagabond behavior and knew perfectly well that if he tried to drive them away there would be an almighty brawl. A brawl on such a happy occasion would be highly inauspicious, all the more so if someone should get killed. But if everything was eaten, what would he offer his guests? All those years of scrimping and saving would have been for nothing.

As they stood there wondering what to do, the vagabonds were getting impatient, banging on the table and yelling, "What's holding up the hot food?"

The host gritted his teeth and ordered the cooks to serve up the fried dishes.

A quick-witted guest whispered to the host that they should send for the county head as soon as they could. The county head would find a way to punish the scoundrels.

That idea cheered everyone up—that's right, the county head was armed and brave—how could a man who had beaten a landlord half to death with a carrying pole be afraid of this pack of low-life bums?

Even as they were getting ready to call for him, the county head was on his way. He was intending to come anyway—he'd been invited some time before to attend as the guest of honor. As befitted his high status, he was showing up a little late. Fortunately not too late—he appeared on the road leading up to the shed just as the hot dishes were being brought out of the kitchen.

For the occasion, the county head was wearing a brand-new Sun Yat-sen suit and an army cap—the most up-to-date wear for officials. The locals had disparaged the dress of the Liberation Army officers just after they arrived in the area as having

little spiky collars,
caps like greasy spoons,
no waist on their baggy pantaloons.

But now the county head had overcome these sartorial deficiencies. To people who still dressed in long gowns over padded trousers, he was an awe-inspiring figure, a crane among chickens. Naturally, what made the county head all the more impressive was the pistol at his waist, decorated with a long tassel that flicked back and forth as he strode along. In his wake were several members of the regional militia, all with rifles on their shoulders.

The county head marched up to where the vagabonds were sitting. He didn't say a word; he simply drew his pistol and weighed it in his hand, as if it were a toy he was holding.

The vagabonds knew they were in trouble when they saw the pistol. They scattered like a flock of birds before the hunter, though not before they had stuffed what remained of the meat and fish into their bags. Those who didn't have time to do that simply grabbed whole plates and took off with them.

The county head lifted his pistol and fired off a few rounds into the air. "Go get 'em!" he shouted. The people hesitated at first, but the sound of his pistol had put as much courage into them as if they'd eaten leopard's gall. They set off in hot pursuit.

But the vagabonds were as practiced in fleeing as they were in thieving. They ran faster than rabbits, and after a long chase not a single one had been captured. All the pursuers had managed to get hold of were the two women who sold bean curd.

Chrysanthemum was local, so they didn't bother to detain

her, but this other one, the Sister, everyone swore blind that she was one of the vagabonds.

So Sister was trussed up and dragged off to county headquarters.

Chrysanthemum pleaded desperately with them, but nobody took any notice of her. The county head snapped, "If you're in so well with her, does that mean that you're teamed up with the robbers?" which terrified Chrysanthemum so badly that she shut her mouth and dared say no more.

Back home, Sister's little girl was screaming with hunger, making Chrysanthemum sadder than ever. Sister had saved her life; how could she stand idly by as Sister herself suffered?

After much soul-searching, she took all the money they had made selling bean curd and spent it on two bottles of liquor. Then she wrapped the bottles carefully in red paper and went off to the boats to find the Priest.

She couldn't think of anyone but him who could save Sister's life. But she had no idea if he would be prepared to help her. So she had to take a gift—if money has the power to make demons turn the mill wheel, a gift like this should at least allow her to say a few words.

To Chrysanthemum's horror, the Priest turned out to be the man with the eyebrows that joined in the middle. Trembling, she handed her gift to him and stumblingly told him her story.

The Priest asked, "Is that Gold Phoenix you're talking about?"

She was taken aback for a moment, then realized that this must be Sister's name, so she nodded vigorously: "Yes, it's her!"

Without even glancing at the humble offering she had brought with her, the Priest agreed to Chrysanthemum's request.

It was cold. The snow that had begun to fall was too light to cover the empty fields and bare trees, but the damp chill in the air cut to the bone. Chrysanthemum curled up in her quilt with the motherless infant, unable to sleep for wondering how the Priest would keep his promise. Would he really be able to save Sister? Then another thought struck her: why had Sister never mentioned that she was Gold Phoenix?

Unknown to Chrysanthemum, the vagabonds had already surrounded county headquarters. Inside the building the county head had loosened his captive's bonds and pushed her down onto the bed.

Sister did not scream or struggle. This was a game that fate was playing with her, and resistance was pointless. She had known that this was so ever since she had come to the Priest and been given the name Gold Phoenix.

Suddenly the door was broken down, and the vagabonds streamed in. The snowy light of their flaming torches lit the two naked bodies on the bed.

The woman did not react with shock—rather she put her hands over her eyes as if bothered by the brightness of the torches. The man was terrified and reached in panic for his trousers. But all his clothes were now in the Priest's hands. "Ha!" he snarled, "so here's the mighty Communist official raping one of our girls!"

The county head pleaded for mercy, his face ashen. The Priest ignored him completely. With a hollow laugh, he ordered Gold Phoenix to get dressed. He had the county head's undershorts in his hand and was squeezing them into a little ball. One of the vagabonds said, "Let's take him to the district office and make an accusation!"

"Fuck that!" The Priest carelessly tossed the undershorts aside. "Officials all look after each other, so what's the use in accusing him?" Tomorrow morning we'll string him up from the flagpole at county headquarters, where everyone can see him."

The vagabonds all clapped and stamped their approval: "Okay, let's string him up right now!"

"We'll haul down the flag and hoist him up instead!"

The county head, still stark naked, listened in abject terror. He'd forgotten all about the gun he had put under the pillow. His official position and Party membership wouldn't save him now. He was finished! He'd have to live as a peasant, working in the fields and eating coarse grain! He couldn't face the thought of so harsh a life—even before Liberation he'd been unable to endure it and had taken up the life of a playboy instead. So, without regard for his dignity, the county head tumbled off the bed and kowtowed to the Priest, his bare bottom sticking up in the air: "Just tell me what you want! I'll do whatever you say!"

The Priest looked at him and grunted softly.

It was as well for the county head that he had learned something of ways of the vagabonds in his playboy days. "Priest," he begged, "let's deal! How much? Just tell me how much!"

Somberly, the Priest raised five dark fingers: "Five hundredweight of rice, not a grain less!"

"Okay, five hundredweight!" The county head nodded jerkily, like a chicken pecking rice. "Now can I have my pants back?"

"Write a note." The Priest wasn't ready to give them back just yet.

So the county head wrote out a requisition order for five hundredweight of rice on official stationery.

The Priest took the order and folded it. "How are you going to deliver it?" he demanded.

"By boat, in three nights, at the second bridge along Gongsun Creek."

The Priest nodded and finally tossed him his undershorts.

When he was dressed, the county head called in the former landlord of the village, gave him a stern political lecture, and commanded him to withdraw five hundredweight of rice, instructing him as to when and where it must be delivered.

By the sacred order of the Priest, Gold Phoenix was taken

back on board, though whether that meant she had been saved was hard to say. As for Chrysanthemum, she could not stay by the river any more because of her connection to Gold Phoenix, so she sold the two-room cottage by the bank that was all she owned and sorrowfully followed Gold Phoenix onto the boats, to live with Sister and her daughter. Everyone on the boats belonged to the same sect, though Chrysanthemum never found out exactly what it was they believed. It wasn't until later, in the "campaign to eliminate counterrevolutionaries," that she discovered the sect was called Yiguandao, "The Way of All Virtue." The Priest was seized by the authorities and executed. The county head denounced Gold Phoenix as a priestess, so she was executed as well. The rest of them were told to go north of the Yangtze to their home villages. Chrysanthemum went along, taking the baby that Sister Gold Phoenix had left with her. She had tried at first to protest that she didn't come from the north, that her home was right there, and that she wasn't even a member of the sect. But she couldn't convince anyone and was left with no choice in the matter.

—5—

As the west wind blew more fiercely, the old bean-curd seller fell ill.

She lay on her bed, looking out through the small high window at a tiny square of sky, a square filled with rain and wind, rain whipped around by the wind and spun into an opaque gray mist. Looking back into her past through years of rain and wind, her own suffering and turmoil seemed misty and vague. Still, there were a few trivial events that floated up from the sea of her memories, clear in every minute detail.

Once she had asked Sister what her name was. Sister was bent low over her washing and didn't even turn her head: "Poor people don't have names worth anything. Puppy, Kitty, Chicken, Bunny—anything will do."

That didn't satisfy Chrysanthemum, so she pressed on: "Didn't the Priest call you Gold Phoenix?"

Sister smiled wryly: "Okay, so I'm Gold Phoenix."

That really puzzled her. She'd never come across anyone who felt that way about her own name. Besides, Sister seemed disgusted, both with the name Gold Phoenix and with the woman who had borne that name. This made her feel that, before she became Gold Phoenix, Sister must have been a different person and lived a different life. How perfect it would be if Sister could be transformed into the child bride that the blind old man longed to find. As far as she knew, Sister had never been married to any of the men on the boat, so the daughter's paternity would always be a mystery.

Maybe Sister and the child bride were nothing to do with each other. There were as many ill-fated women in the world as there were hairs on a cow's back. Take herself—hadn't she also ended up on the boats? Vast though the world may be, the roads that its inhabitants are forced to travel are narrow and constrained. Only misfortune penetrates every corner and leaves its traces everywhere.

Again and again she returned to her thoughts of the past and wondered whether to tell the blind man about Sister. She realized that, old and sick as she was, she had little time left. It would make little difference to her whether she told him or not, but there was her daughter to be considered. Fragrance was the infant that Sister had left in her care some forty years before, and she had hidden the girl's origin from the world all that time, hidden it even from Fragrance herself. From the time she was relocated to the north, she had told everyone that Fragrance was her own daughter and that the girl's father had drowned.

Enduring countless hardships, she had devoted herself to raising the girl. Fragrance understood how hard her mother's life was and worked hard in school, always coming out at the top of the class. In the third year of high school, a boy in her class wrote her a love letter comparing her to a flower. She was too shy to tell anyone about the letter or even to give it back, so she tore it up and pretended that nothing had happened. But she couldn't keep herself from glancing in the mirror and seeing that her black eyes sparkled with life, that the complexion of her oval face was unblemished, that her dimples were deep and her lips red . . . then her heart would pound, and she would push the mirror aside and chide herself for this "unhealthy sentimentalism."

Even so, she knew from the looks that others gave her that she was beautiful. She was gratified by this, though she didn't place too high a value on these gifts. Schoolwork was more important to her. With such good grades, it was natural that she wanted to take university entrance examinations, but this also caused her some anxiety. Her mother had sacrificed so much to see her through high school—how could she expect her to manage all the expenses for university as well? How could the poor woman ever afford it?

But then, on the eve of her graduation from high school, the Liberation Army's Foreign Language School came to recruit students. At schools of this kind, all expenses were met by the state. Overjoyed, she went at once to see her teacher and told her she wanted to sign up. The teacher disapproved, feeling that so excellent a student should go to university. When she went to see the girl's mother, she found the woman was not keen either. Chrysanthemum didn't want the girl to leave her, preferring to have her marry and bring a son-in-law into their family.

Fragrance applied anyway and met the chief of the Regional Military Bureau, who had accompanied the recruiting officers to examine the applicants personally. Fragrance passed the political and physical tests and waited excitedly for notice of her admission. But when the day came for the new students to be going off to school, others were summoned, and she was left behind.

Word went around that there had been some problem concerning Fragrance's class origins and that she had been turned down for political reasons. That seemed to be the only possible explanation—otherwise, how could such an outstanding student be barred from entering a military college? But then, as she was lamenting her fate, she received a summons to an audience with the chief of the Military Bureau. Her eyes were still full of tears as she went into his office. But he said, "You shouldn't listen to gossip. We did check up on you, but there's no problem with your background. Your mother is a genuine poor peasant. We kept you here for the needs of the revolution! How about it, little fighter! Come here to the Military Bureau. We need people like you to carry on our work!" Fragrance had never expected this. She was relieved but still couldn't help feeling a twinge of disappointment. She had wanted to go on with her studies so badly.

Her mother was so delighted with the news that she got up in the middle of the night to offer secret thanks to the Buddha. The way she saw it, her daughter could both remain by her side and get out of being registered as a peasant. What an honor it was for someone so young to be selected for work at regional headquarters! Soon enough she'd be able to find a worthy young man for her daughter to marry, and she could live out her life secure and content.

Fragrance saw how happy her mother was and couldn't bring herself to protest. It was a job, after all, and would relieve the burden on her mother. So she went to work at regional headquarters. She was assigned to perform clerical duties at the office of the chief of the Military Bureau, effectively acting as his secretary. She learned the work quickly and did well at it. The bureau chief praised her highly and called her "Little Fragrance." Since he thought well of her, so did everyone else at the office. Taking their cue from the chief, they all called her Little Fragrance as well.

Life smiled on Fragrance, scattering rose petals in her path.

Soon the chief offered to sponsor her for membership in the Communist Party, even though she was only eighteen. She was young and beautiful and had good prospects—she couldn't believe her luck. Her disappointment at missing out on university had already evaporated.

Since her home was too far from headquarters for her to get back every night, she stayed in the office workers' hostel. If any important document or phone message came in, she would go straight over to the chief's house to report it.

The chief's house was very quiet. His son was married and living away from home. Only the chief and his wife remained, occupying three rather spacious rooms. His wife was around fifty; she was from Shandong and had bound feet. Fragrance had been very struck by this fact at their first meeting, and though she had done her best not to stare, she couldn't help giving those feet a second glance. The chief's wife didn't take offense. Instead, she pushed a foot forward and remarked, "Haven't seen this often, have you, lassie? It was pretty feudal where I came from!"

Hearing her accent, Fragrance started to address her, in Shandong fashion, as "Nanny." Nanny was a good-hearted woman; she was very sympathetic when she heard that Fragrance had lost her father as a child and been raised by her widowed mother. If Fragrance came by with a letter at mealtime, she would insist that the girl eat with them. When she was preparing dumplings, she would make a point of inviting the girl over. Fragrance was quick and skillful: if she saw that there were chores that needed to be done, she would go ahead with them, just as she would in her own home.

Nanny was an expert seamstress, but not very good at knitting. She had been working on a sweater for the chief for months, but it still had no sleeves. Fragrance took it away and had it finished in three days. It looked smart and stylish, and Nanny was so pleased she told everyone about it. If the chief was away on business, Nanny would invite Fragrance over to keep her company, and she got Fragrance to help her when she went shopping, as though they were mother and daughter. The neighbors flattered her: "You're so lucky to have such a lovely girl." Someone suggested, "Really, Fragrance, you should be addressing her as Foster Mother." Nanny's eyes crinkled into a loving smile: "I don't know that I could ever be that lucky!" So Fragrance sweetly said, "Foster Mother." Nanny was shocked at first, but delighted as well, and quickly acknowledged the girl's greeting.

The old woman was beside herself with joy. That evening she brought out the sweater that Fragrance had knitted and told the chief to try it on: "Our girl knitted it. See if it fits!"

It was fine, of course. Light and elastic, it fitted perfectly on his broad chest, better by far than the barrel-shaped ones that his wife had made for him. But the Chief still found fault with his wife: "We're comrades in the army of the revolution—what's the idea of calling her a foster daughter!"

Nanny was so cowed that she dared not say a word. The chief turned on Fragrance: "Taking foster children is a feudal tradition! Party members like us don't go in for this kind of nonsense. Comradeship is the closest bond for us."

Fragrance turned away and grimaced at Nanny. She went on calling her Foster Mother, but only when the chief wasn't around, and Nanny answered readily to the name.

The chief announced that he would be away on business for a couple of days, and Nanny invited Fragrance over as she usually did. Then after lunch, she took a tumble. It wasn't too bad a fall, but it was just as well Fragrance was there to call a car and get her to the hospital. It seemed from the examination that there might be some complications, and she would have to stay in the hospital for further observation. Fragrance helped with the admission procedures, nursing the patient, bringing food, fetching and carrying what she needed. It was late in the evening before she was finished, by which time the office compound was locked and she couldn't get into her room. So she went to the chief's house.

No sooner had she gone to bed than she heard the door. The chief was back. Actually he hadn't gone far at all, just visiting a nearby commune.

Fragrance was taken aback and confused about what she should do. The chief reassured her: "Don't worry. You can stay here, and I'll sleep in the study."

The chief had an army cot set up in the next room. But, for some reason, Fragrance still had a sense of foreboding. She could feel her own heart thumping and was at a loss to understand why she should be frightened. In the stillness she could hear the soft sounds of the chief undressing, the clink of the buckle on his army belt, and the scrape of a match being lit. It began to dawn on her that she was afraid of the silent darkness, of sleeping in the next room to a man. She began to regret staying here to sleep, but where else was there for her to go? If he were awake, how could she explain it to him? She couldn't say, "I'm frightened of you." How would that sound? What would the chief think of that?

She tossed and turned on the bed, lying awake for ages, feeling that the blackness was a pit that threatened to swallow her. Unconsciously she clenched her fists, preparing to do battle with imaginary perils. But nothing happened but the scrape of the chief striking another match in the next room. Gradually the tension relaxed, to be replaced by a sense of sadness. She was sorry for herself—she should now be a university student basking in beautiful dreams, not lying in someone else's house shaking with nerves. How much better it would have been to go to university than have nothing to look forward to but a monotonous life pushing papers and answering the phone.

This was the first time since starting work that she had felt anxiety about her future, and even she was surprised at how sudden and painful this anxiety was.

Years later, when she looked back on this moment, she realized that in that evening her young heart had had a premonition of the misery that lay before her.

At the time, she could acknowledge no such thing. Her intellect suppressed those stubborn subconscious fears that refused to go away. The chief and his wife were so good to her, they treated her like a daughter. Her job was undemanding, leaving her with time to study on her own—she could even take the university entrance exams next year if the chief would let her . . . what was there to worry about?

The sound of even breathing came from the next room. She relaxed, feeling ashamed of herself. The chief was an old revolutionary, a higher-up; how could she have been suspicious of him? Clearly it was her own political consciousness that was at fault, making her susceptible to absurd imaginings. No wonder the chief had said that her application to join the Party still needed "thorough consideration"!

At last she fell into a deep sleep and saw in her dreams a beautiful garden. In it grew marvelous flowers and extraordinary plants that she had never seen before. She went in to smell the flowers. Then suddenly the weather changed; dark clouds filled the sky, and everything before her went black, hot rain pelting down like molten lava. She ran in terror, but she couldn't escape. The rain was getting hotter and hotter, searing her flesh. She was suffocating from the heat. As she struggled for her life, she realized that she was actually being held down by a man's powerful hands. She tried to scream, but one of those hands covered her mouth: "Don't make a sound! If anyone hears, we're both finished!"

It was the chief's voice. She was paralyzed with horror. He took the opportunity to hold her more tightly still, murmuring all the time how dear she was to him, how he yearned for her to give herself to him just once. Barely aware of what he was saying, she pushed at him instinctively, desperate to escape. The chief hissed, "So you want to make a fuss, do you? Well, see if I care! What kind of a future do you think you'd have?"

Terror-stricken, she started to struggle again, but she dared not go too far, dared not make a noise. She was afraid the neighbors might hear. When it was over, she cried, but even her sobbing was muffled, very soft, for fear of being heard.

When she went to work the next morning, her eyes were swollen. Her colleagues asked her what was wrong, and she told them she had the flu. The following Sunday at home, she just stared blankly ahead, unable to eat or sleep. Chrysanthemum was worried sick. Assuming that her daughter was suffering from overwork, she called the doctor and busied herself all day preparing nourishing things for her daughter to eat. On Monday Fragrance went back to the office.

For a full week she didn't go to the chief's house. Then he called to say that his wife was back from the hospital and wanted to see her. Afraid that people would be suspicious if she did not go, she gritted her teeth and went over.

He hadn't been lying. Nanny really was back. But when Fragrance entered the house, the chief summoned her into his study straight away, rather than letting her chat with Nanny in the living room as she had in the past. As she went in, he shut the door and put his arms around her. Ashamed and afraid, she screamed out, "Foster Mother! Help!"

Nanny had no idea what was going on. She hobbled into the room on her tiny bound feet, pushed the study door open, and stared in horror at the sight before her. The chief twisted around and snapped, "Get out of here! It's none of your business!"

Eyes downcast, Nanny shuffled out, pulling the door to as she went, submissive as a chastened child bride.

Smirking, the chief lifted Fragrance off her feet, carried her out through the living room to the bedroom, where he laid her down on the bed.

That was the second time.

And then it happened again, the third time, a fourth time. . . . The people at her office seemed to know; they gossiped about her behind her back but couldn't do so publicly for fear of the chief's power. In the spring she wrote her declaration of intent to join the Party, and the authorities passed it. Her colleagues came to congratulate her, their looks a mixture of fawning and contempt. In her mind, life was just a series of disasters—better to have done with it all! But as she walked along the river, she saw the fish swimming happily, the lilacs about to burst into bloom. Life was so good! How could she die!

Another month went by. The chief was no longer bothering her, and hope began to revive in her heart. She thought that the chief might have had a change of heart, so she stealthily retrieved all the textbooks she had studied before and studied in her room at the hostel after work. She could put her name down for the entrance exams that summer; that way she could be far from here and get away from the chief forever.

One April afternoon, the office compound was carpeted with willow floss, and the kind of warm southerly breeze was blowing that makes people light-headed. It was still light after work, so Fragrance took a book down to the riverbank behind the compound.

"Fragrance!" She lifted her head and saw the chief blocking her path. "Where are you going?" he asked amiably. "The canteen will be opening soon."

"Oh, I have food. I bought extra at lunch," she explained hastily. Actually it was only a couple of cold rolls. She seldom went for a hot meal in the evening.

"It's not good for you just to have cold rolls. Come round to my place and eat dumplings." She knew all too well what this meant—any food, no matter how coarse, would taste better to her than those dumplings ever could. But she dared not refuse his invitation, and she could not escape him. Without his consent, she could not even apply for the university entrance examinations.

When they got to the house, the chief pushed a sheet of paper toward her. It was his divorce from the Shandong woman. She knew then that all hope was lost.

She and the chief were married at the end of April. He was thirty years her senior.

Even after the divorce, the woman from Shandong stayed on in the house—there was nowhere else for her to go, and the chief couldn't simply kick her out onto the street. She still made dumplings and did the laundry, cooking, and cleaning for the chief, but she did not call Fragrance "our girl" any more.

Then in June, the Cultural Revolution started. The first big-character poster at the Military Bureau was headlined "SEE HOW THE DAUGHTER OF THE HEAD OF A REACTIONARY SECT SEDUCES AND CORRUPTS A REVOLUTIONARY CADRE!"

Fragrance was dragged outside. The lustrous hair was shaved off one side of her head; a string of stinking old shoes, symbols of prostitution, was hung around her neck. She was dragged around town on a rope. Chrysanthemum heard the news and rushed in from the village. This docile and submissive peasant woman, who had borne so much hardship without complaint, suddenly turned into a tigress fighting for her cub. Her hair on end, she stormed into the office compound with a handful of stones, which she hurled at all the windows. As the glass smashed, she screamed, "My family has been poor landless peasants for eighteen generations! And Fragrance is my own flesh! If you don't believe me, cut her open, and see her blood!"

As a crowd of onlookers gathered, the old woman kept going: "Chairman Mao! Chairman Mao! Our class enemies are revenging themselves, conspiring against poor peasants, persecuting my 'five red element' daughter! . . ."

Chrysanthemum really was a poor peasant, so the revolutionary rebels couldn't just kick her out. It was also the case that the poster was based on hearsay, without much in the way of hard fact, and was written by people whose own class origin wasn't any too sound, certainly by comparison with Chrysanthemum's. So the "reactionary sect" affair fizzled out. In place of the first poster, a new one went up, with a revised headline: "THE CAPITALIST ROADER, FICKLE IN HIS AFFECTIONS, IS DECADENT AND CORRUPT!"

On this poster, the chief's name was written upside down, with red crosses slashed through the characters of his name. So the chief wrote a hasty rebuttal in a poster of his own—Fragrance certainly was from a reactionary sect; he had seen it in her dossier. He went on to document how he been smitten by this temptress from an enemy class, how she had seduced and corrupted him, how he would strive to make amends for his past transgressions, how he would draw a dividing line between himself and this white-bone demon disguised as a beauty . . . and more in the same vein.

He was as good as his word, divorcing Fragrance and remarrying the woman from Shandong. After the divorce, Fragrance was locked away in a "cowshed" and interrogated constantly. As for the chief, he was quickly restored to power by virtue of his excellent attitude.

Like all organizations in those days, the Military Bureau had two principal revolutionary mass organizations competing for power, and the chief was the head of one of them. In one skirmish, his faction scored a decisive victory, inflicting heavy casualties on his enemies. Then suddenly a new directive came down from on high that seemed to work on the defeated faction like an elixir, bringing them miraculously to life. Seeking revenge for their fallen comrades, they demanded that the chief be dragged out and put on public trial.

When news of this reached the chief, he fled by night to a secret hideaway and kept out of sight. When the rival faction couldn't find him, they hauled Fragrance out of the cowshed to struggle with her instead. Several struggle sessions went by, and they still didn't feel sufficiently revenged, so someone suggested a plan: one of the ways the reactionary sects had exercised their tyranny in the past was to throw people into a vat of acid and send them up to heaven in a puff of smoke. Why not do the same thing to this woman right now? That would be a condemnation of the reactionary sects and revenge for the martyrs to the cause!

So they set about preparing a vat of nitric acid. When the woman from Shandong found out what was going on, she hobbled over to where the chief was hiding and pleaded with him to find a way to save the girl. But he had no intention of helping her. "I'm like a clay Buddha crossing a river," he told his wife. "It's all I can do to save myself." The coldness in his tone showed his anger at her for coming to see him—it would be no joke if his hiding place were discovered! The old woman sighed and left. But she didn't go home—she hobbled out of town until, her feet covered with blisters, she found Fragrance's mother, Chrysanthemum.

In the middle of the night, Chrysanthemum set fire to the woodpile behind the cowshed where her daughter was imprisoned. In the confusion that ensued, she rescued the girl and led her to a waiting boat. In the twinkling of an eye, they had vanished without a trace, just as the vagabonds had done in their day.

They never went back. The news reached them that the chief had got his job back again and gone on to still higher things, being promoted to assistant commissioner at the district office. One sunny day ten years later, Fragrance was at a waste retrieval depot to sell the scraps she had collected. Sorting them into categories, she noticed a piece of an old newspaper, with a photograph of a familiar face. When she picked it up, she saw that it was a picture of herself at age eighteen. Under the photograph was a missing persons notice. The chief—or rather the assistant commissioner—was searching for her, claiming her as his wife, and stating that the divorce pronounced during the Ten Years of Chaos was invalid.

The girl at the depot hurried her along: "Five pounds of glass, two of feathers, paper . . . get a move on!" Hastily she folded the page and tossed it in with the rest of the scrap paper. And from that time, another ten years had passed.

The fiddle played on incessantly, the hand that guided the bow trembling, so that the music quivered and the melody became discordant, like a whimper or a groan.

To the unrelenting accompaniment of the fiddle, Chrysanthemum approached the brink of death. Her daughter had stopped selling bean curd, waiting day and night at the bedside. The blind man no longer told the women his own life story, nor did he ask them for theirs. He just sat in the doorway, the fiddle always in his hand.

The light in Chrysanthemum's eyes grew fainter day by day. She still felt as if she were in a little boat, bobbing up and down on the water. Life just bobs along until it's finished, with no discernable reason. The day her daughter helped her down from the boat she had said, "Ma, it'll be fine here." Alarmed and disconcerted, she had looked around her and realized that this place, so strange and yet so familiar, was the village in which she had been born. Under this earth lay the bodies of her parents, her husband, and the pitiful woman she had called Sister. In all the years that she and her daughter had kept on the move, she had never consciously thought of coming home. There was too much sadness buried here; she did not want to dig it up again. Yet when they were on the water, she would always sit up at the prow of the boat and tell her daughter, "We're southbound, southbound. . . ." The reason she gave was that she wanted to get nearer the big cities, where they would do better business with their bean curd. She had no sense of the mystic force drawing her back to her roots.

At the beginning she had been a little worried that people might recognize her and harm her daughter. But she soon had reason to feel reassured. "Time is money"—that was the spirit of the age, and people were too busy with their own business to give her a second glance. As a girl she had been lovely as a flower, but she had held no interest for men for many years. Better to say that "time is a curtain" separating the stages in a person's life, changing appearances beyond recognition. This was something Chrysanthemum understood as well as anyone.

One moonlit night, she went furtively to the place where her home had been. Where once that thatched cottage had stood was a two-story house with painted horses adorning the walls and lights burning upstairs and down. The day she had left this house, the line of peach trees had been in blossom; she went all around the house to look, though she knew the peach trees wouldn't be there any more. She trembled with fright as the songs of the Taiwanese pop singer Theresa Teng came gushing out from the windows. Realizing her stealth would make her look like a thief, she crept wretchedly away.

Suddenly she had a flash of the village schoolmaster reciting a poem, his head bobbing up and down as he spoke:

"Bright is the moon, the stars are few,
Crows and sparrows southward fly.
Three times they circle round a tree,
No branch whereon to roost they spy."

How like her own life that sounded! Was she not like one of those birds in the poem, flying south to her home, but with no place there for her to perch or roost? Yet even though she had nowhere to roost, she still had to return, to die on familiar soil. Humans are a conundrum that they themselves can never solve.

How could she know that when she returned to the village where her family had lived for generations, she would find herself lodging with a poor blind man from some distant place? She had never seen this blind man before and decided that he must have settled here after she had gone north. If only the blind man had come here earlier, or if Sister's tragedy had happened later, then they might have been able to control their own earthly destinies; but they had never met again. A human life is like a speck of rice chaff swept along by swift summer streams, helpless to control where it will go.

What good would it have done them if Gold Phoenix and the blind man had met, even if she had made his dream come true by being Bunny? This kindly blind man could not have saved Gold Phoenix and Fragrance from their cruel fates, and his inability to help them would have burdened him with a guilt even more terrible than his futile lifelong quest. . . .

When Chrysanthemum recovered from her reverie, she started to speak several times, but always bit back her words. She was ready for death, but her daughter was younger, still in her forties. She believed that, no matter how the political climate had changed, her daughter was still safer as the child of a poor peasant rather than of a woman executed for membership in a reactionary cult . . . in the last moment of her consciousness, she held her daughter's hand tightly, her withered lips opening and closing weakly. "Mother," the daughter asked, "what is it you want to tell me?" She answered, "When I'm gone, I won't rest easy if I leave you on your own. This blind uncle is such a good man, and he's walked more bridges than you have roads. He's suffered even more than we have; adopt each other as father and daughter; then you'll each have someone to care for you. You can even get a household registration and settle here."

"Mother!" the daughter turned pale, as if all this had caught her by surprise.

The blind man also came out of his daze and pricked up his ears. He was so tense his temples began to throb. These past days he had never lost hope, always believing that this old bean-curd seller was really Bunny, even though she had never talked about her past. He saw in her silence cause for hope—if she weren't Bunny, she need have no misgivings, so why not say so? There must be some reason, too painful to disclose, that prevented her from revealing her true identity. No matter—heaven had blessed them by allowing them to meet again at the end of their lives. He stayed all night outside her door, playing his fiddle one last time as the autumn wind whistled to send her on her way. Hearing her make this last charge to her daughter, he felt more than ever that he had been right. Suddenly he realized—he needed to have a daughter, and now he had one! His heart bursting with emotions that he could not voice, he waited. . . .

The daughter didn't understand. She didn't want to do what her mother had told her to. She felt that she had no other family in the world than her mother, with whom she had endured so much. But the old woman's deathbed wishes could not be denied. This woman had borne her, raised her, loved and protected her, and must now be allowed to close her eyes in peace . . . the daughter brought to her mother's bedside the old man who had waited so long at her door and softly and painfully spoke the words "Foster Father!"

Chrysanthemum finally closed her eyes. In her confused mind, she believed she had done the best she could for her daughter, that nobody would again think of throwing her in a vat of acid. She had found her daughter a tiny haven in a tempestuous world.

Blind Old Pots' heart was soaring, scarcely daring to believe the scene before him, as if he were looking down from the clouds on a mirage of Atlantis. . . .

At last his hopes had been fulfilled. Even if he were to die at that moment, he would be perfectly content. Fragrance had called him Foster Father, but he would call her daughter, my new daughter, my own dear girl. He wouldn't dwell in the past any more, just concentrate on living with his daughter. He fumbled around to light the fire for Fragrance and even insisted on turning the grindstone for her—nothing she could say would hold him back. One day he took apart the ragged pillow he always slept on and drew out three silver coins, all the money that he had saved in a lifetime of begging and balladry. He handed it to Fragrance: "Daughter, fate has been unkind to me. I've been poor all my life; I didn't see you through your first months; I never raised you or cared for you. Take this money and have some clothes made!"

Fragrance took the money in silence. The next day she went out and bought the blind man a smart new twill suit. Pots was choked with sobs as he scolded her: "Silly girl! Silly girl!" But his tears were tears of joy, the only joyful tears that had ever flowed from his sightless eyes.

No grief is greater than a heart that's died,
No greater joy than longings satisfied.

Heaven had taken pity on Pots. He had everything now that he had always longed for; he must never lose it again.

Pots woke up one morning to an extraordinary stillness. He sat up in alarm, straining to hear those familiar little morning sounds, but in vain. He hurried from his bed and groped clumsily around the two rooms of his cottage. He discovered a sack of soybeans and a bowl of bean curd left out on top of the stove. Under the bowl was a sheet of paper. Everything else—the grindstone, Fragrance's bedding roll—was gone. He took the note to a neighbor to find out what it said. The man read it three times, but still Pots couldn't seem to understand. Impatiently, the man tossed the note back: "Okay, so they're checking up on tax evasion, and this woman's never paid any tax, so the brigade wants to make an example of her. She's going to get fined, so she takes off. Understand?"

"That's not fair," someone said sympathetically. "She can't have made much selling bean curd; how's she expected to pay a fine?"

"There's lots of people don't pay tax," someone else added. "Who's ever seen any of the new rich households paying tax? They're just picking on her because she's not from round here."

"She was too honest. If she'd just paid off the Party secretary, there'd have been no mention of tax."

"It's not honesty that's her problem, it's age—if she'd been twenty years younger. . . ."

There was some nervous giggling in the group that had gathered round. The blind man shook slightly; then he turned and walked away.

He shouldn't have given Fragrance those three silver dollars to buy clothes; if he'd only got the money now, she could have paid off the fine. Then she wouldn't have had to leave.

He walked along Slanting Brook. The water was down, there were mudflats at the bend in the river, and stone steps to the bridges that were usually submerged were now exposed, cracked and crumbling under mosses and lichen. Dead reeds rustled in the wind, and geese honked in the barren wastes as they flew south.

Suddenly from downriver he heard the clatter of nets being thrown over the sides of fishing boats. Pots stood still, imagining the fish darting here and there, some of them swimming into the nets and being tangled up, some slipping through the mesh and getting away. Those unfortunate enough to be caught would never again be returned to their riverbed world. Their tragedy was that generation after generation, big and small, fat and thin, adult and immature, all knew that there were nets set out to snare them but swam right into them just the same. In the pitiful clans of fishdom, who knew how many times the grief of a family destroyed had been repeated?

Unconsciously he picked up his fiddle, thinking of playing some tune or other, but before a note had been played, his hands dropped to his sides in dejection—it was too late now for the song from *Two at the Grindstone,* and he had no songs to share with his daughter. Daughter . . . she had never once called him Dad, or even Foster Father after that one time. When she had been excitedly getting him to try on his new clothes, she had called him "Uncle." "Uncle" and "Dad" were worlds apart, but he hadn't wanted to listen to the words. In his own mind he had been a father for a few days, though his daughter had been a mystery to him. He had never known a thing about her world.

They say that people who are parted will meet again, but they may not always know each other when they do! Sometimes they are kept apart by the silence of heavy stones. Hearts are deep sealed wells, with no links between them. Perhaps in days to come, when heaven and earth grow old, secret underground streams will force their way through, but human life is too short to wait for that time to come.

He walked on, confused, the past a dream. Perhaps he'd never had a daughter at all. Perhaps Bunny had never existed. Perhaps it had all been an illusion. And now he was walking in a dream.

But there were sounds he could hear clearly—the popping of puffed rice, the calls of the sellers of preserved ginger, the gongs of the dealers exchanging candies for scraps, the chant of the buyers of rabbit fur, a boat being poled through the water, the quack of ducks let out onto the water.

They would never catch all the fish in the river, and the waters would never run dry. A huge yellow sun sank down below the earth, and the warm clouds of evening flooded the river. But still Pots shivered, as the west wind sent a chill through his body. Struggling to stop himself from shaking, he took up his fiddle again, dragging his bow back and forth across the strings as he sang:

"Pots sings to tell his tale,
Pots plays for me.
Add the master to us both,
and people there are three. . . ."

He sang of Bunny, of his daughter, of how they had been reunited only for him to lose them again. But his voice slurred, the song made no sense, and the fiddle wept hoarsely, a dirty yellow stream of polluted sound.

Nobody could make head nor tail of his song.

"The blind man's off his head again!" they said.

Street Sketch

I go out of my door early to find a crowd of people at the street corner. The Shanghainese are notorious for their curiosity—if one person stoops to look at a dead ant on the road, someone else will join him, then a third and a fourth. Soon, dozens, even hundreds of people will press round. If you didn't know what was going on, you might assume that a space alien had landed in the city!

I decide to walk around them, but my attention is caught by a rasping voice: "Grandfathers, uncles, tradesmen, young friends, one and all! I am a disciple of Master Haideng, the great exponent of the martial arts! I come here today to this corner of your fair city, not in search of personal gain, but to bring good fortune to all. . . ."

The last few years we have seen a big increase in the number of people peddling quack medicines. They start with a catchy come-on spiel, then they strip to the waist and do stunts, and finally they bring out their elixir and hit you for money. We weren't born yesterday. We're not so easily fooled into buying pills, powders, pastes, and pellets concocted from heaven knows what kinds of greasy filth and foot-washing water. Still, for all that, there's something rather entertaining

Translated by Wendy Lambert and Richard King

about watching someone swallow nails or drill a hole through a brick with his finger. So when you see one of these guys starting his sales pitch, you stick around to watch, even though you know how the show is going to end. Then what do you do when the performance is over and the outstretched hand comes your way? Like they say up north: no way, eh?

But this guy starts a little differently from the others, claiming off the top, truthfully or otherwise, that he's here to bring us all good fortune. He wears a pair of baggy black trousers held up by a filthy red sash and is naked from the waist up, with arms as thin as hemp stalks and a chest so scrawny you can count the ribs. His face has a ravenous look, and his stomach caves in like a well. He looks like he hasn't had a decent meal in years.

"I am Sichuanese." He holds up an envelope with a line of characters printed on it, shaking it in our direction: "See, here's my address—Ma Family Village, Tianqiao County, Yongli District, Sichuan Province. If you're ever in Sichuan, just ask the first person you meet, 'Where is Longlife Ma of Ma Family Village?' Anyone will tell you. . . ."

Even in the unlikely event of there being another Sichuanese in the crowd to disprove his claim, I'd still be prepared to bet that 99 percent of the people here aren't going to believe a word of it.

Then his sales pitch takes an abrupt turn, as he pulls from his pocket a small paper package. As he walks around the semicircle of onlookers, he begins to unwrap it, showing everyone a few grains of white powder in their paper wrapping. "If I told you that this medicine was guaranteed to cure any illness, you certainly wouldn't believe me. Just bragging won't do any good—that would be like trying to build Mount Tai by piling up dirt. But if you don't believe me now, I can make you believe! How? With facts! Facts will show that there is a marvelous power at work in this powder, and this power is qigong! You must have heard of qigong. . . ."

Now it's obvious—he thinks we're stupid. We Shanghainese have seen a lot; we know more than he realizes. Who is there that hasn't heard fanciful stories about the wonderful powers of qigong? And it isn't just qigong stories we've heard—there's also stuff about people who can read with their ears or bring things through solid walls by willpower, extraterrestrials captured by Soviet scientists, and prehistoric television sets excavated from the Pyramids. To say nothing of yin and yang, the Eight Trigrams and the Book of Changes!

People sneer at the little Sichuanese. He waves dismissively: "You should certainly have heard of the great qigong master Yan Xin! Who is Yan Xin, you ask? He is a famous professor at Sichuan Medical College! There's an essay all about him in the March issue of *Flower City* magazine, a hundred thousand characters long." His eyes gleam with excitement. "I want to tell you about Yan Xin's powers. It is plainly stated in that essay that he can remove a mole from someone's face at a distance of fifteen hundred kilometers! If he's giving a lecture and he tells you to laugh, you'll laugh. If he tells you to cry, you'll cry. If he tells you to jump, you'll jump. . . .

"What's the secret behind these great truths? It can't be explained in two or three words, but . . ."—he clears his throat and continues in stentorian tones—". . . 'Qigong is a higher science, an anatomical science, an advanced technology. . . .' I'm not making this up, you know; those are the words of the great scientist Qian Xuesen! And all that advanced technology is in this medicine! This medicine is a special cure for all chronic illnesses! Men and women, old and young, all can have chronic illnesses. Babies suffer malnutrition and roundworm, children get indigestion, old folks have dizzy spells and can't control their bladders, women have irregular periods and menstrual cramps, middle-aged men are impotent or ejaculate prematurely, even youngsters. . . ."

He pauses a moment, then sounds his words out more clearly than ever: "Young men have a malady known as 'marrying in your dreams.'. . . Why do we call it 'marrying in your dreams'? Because it afflicts a man who has yet to marry but longs for a wife day and night. When evening comes, he has a dream—that he is with a woman! How happy he feels! How wonderful if he could only have this dream every night! But. . . ."

"Friends!" He slaps his thigh, and his voice becomes ferocious: "If you have that dream every night, you will be ruined forever! When you get up, your head will swim, your back will ache, and your joints will be weak. And when you finally do get married, you're no good for anything! But to those who have such dreams I say that help is at hand. If you take my medicine, you will never again have a wife in your dreams. Instead you will really marry! A beautiful young virgin! I guarantee it!"

Laughter ripples through the crowd. The atmosphere has changed; now everyone feels amused and relaxed. Then he takes out a bundle of envelopes. "I have twenty envelopes here, which I will give to twenty people. People who get envelopes are getting my medicine free of charge. All I ask is that, once you have taken it, you send me testimonies to its effectiveness. This is so that I can improve it still further. The address is on the envelopes. I have only twenty! Once they're gone, there won't be any more! Okay, who wants one?"

Craning his scrawny neck, he turns his head to scrutinize every individual in the crowd. Nobody says anything, but many of them crane their necks and widen their eyes or else shuffle their feet and hope that the others won't notice. Some stroke their chins or clear their throats for no apparent reason.

The Sichuanese gives a little cough himself to ease the tension: "Folks from Shanghai are a bit, well . . . okay, I'll make it easier for you. If you want one, raise your hand!"

Almost before the words are out, a trendy-looking youngster in Nike running shoes gives a half-mocking laugh and raises his hand in a kind of salute. Then, as if roused by a clarion call, more hands go up, some high, some low; some urgently, others diffidently. The momentum seems to sweep people up. A plump middle-aged woman near me lifts her right arm ever so slightly, then drops it down again. But, to my astonishment, he goes straight over to her and offers her the first envelope!

Many of the onlookers are taken aback, not least the young man in the Nikes, who scowls and begins to grumble. The Sichuanese laughs: "Don't fret, young fellow. I know this lady believes in me, even if she didn't raise her hand. She needs my medicine!"

The plump woman blushes. With a smile he asks her, "Are you a Party member, Ma'am?"

Though his voice is scarcely above a whisper, she's obviously extremely embarrassed. But he just smiles: "It's all right. None of your leaders are here. It's okay for us to have a little chat."

People begin to laugh. The woman's face turns red, then white, but she still reaches out and takes the envelope. In smooth, measured tones, the Sichuanese continues: "The Party calls on us to serve the people, and that's exactly what I do. As to the question of whether qigong is materialism or idealism, well, let's deal with that another time. People from Shanghai are all well informed—I'm sure you all know that American president Ronald Reagan is a firm believer in astrology. What you may not know is that the supreme leaders of our own country also use divination to set state policy and lead the Chinese revolution from one victory to another. This is not superstition! It is an irrefutable truth in Marxist philosophy that spirit is transformed into substance and substance is transformed into spirit. Qigong is substance that has been spiritualized. . . ."

Swindler he may be, but he's good—you have to give him credit for that!

One by one the envelopes are handed out and carefully held open to catch a few grains of the white powder that he shakes in. You can see from their expressions that the recipients are delighted.

When he has finished doling out the medicine, the Sichuanese unexpectedly taps a thin man on the shoulder: "Friend, I've talked so much my lips are dry and my mouth is parched. Can you give me fifty cents for an ice cream?"

The thin man is neatly dressed and wears a pair of old-fashioned tortoiseshell-frame glasses. In his string shopping bag are some vegetables and a small white fish. He looks like an average kind of intellectual, struggling to make ends meet, and maybe a bit henpecked too, and he dithers anxiously over the prospect of parting with fifty cents. He doesn't hesitate for long before the rest of the crowd starts to grumble indignantly at the Sichuanese, feeling that he's trying to hoodwink them. The plump woman moves quickest; without a word, she spins round like a girl of eighteen. The youth in Nikes is close behind her, slipping away as though his soles were greased. All at once, everyone wants out of there.

At this, the expression on the face of the Sichuanese changes. Suddenly he bellows, "Listen! All of you! Who is there, in today's society, who can catch a white tiger?"

I can't understand what he's talking about. In the confusion, an old woman whispers, "What's he mean about catching white tigers?" She shakes her head. An old man, maybe a retired worker, pushes his way back through the crowd to explain: "Catching a white tiger is getting something for nothing." Smugly he adds, "I caught on right away. There's no way you can get something for nothing. Sure this guy's full of fine words, but he still asks for money in the end, doesn't he?"

The old woman nods agreement. Neither of them has received envelopes, so they aren't in any hurry to leave. But I remember that they were craning their necks hopefully with the rest when the medicine was being handed out.

"You! And you!" The Sichuanese jerks his hands up—first

the left, then the right—to point at the retreating figures of the plump woman and the youngster in Nikes.

I can't really explain that gesture of his, but everyone understands it instantly. As if compelled by some mysterious force, they are frozen in their tracks. Everyone stops dead. Nobody dares move. And those two, the man and the woman, tremble convulsively, unable to control themselves or take a step.

"I'm not forcing anyone to stay." The voice softens slightly. "But I tell you this—you can go all the way to America, and you'll still be in my grasp. Makes no difference if you believe me. . . ." He claps his hands twice. "I can make your head hurt when you read or your stomach ache when you eat. I can make you rush to the bathroom and then find you can't piss. When you're right there on top of a woman I can stop you getting it off. . . ."

He points again. The plump woman and the youngster in Nikes come back, step by step.

It's unbelievable. In the bustle of the world, there's suddenly an abyss of silence, like a black hole, like a whirlpool in the Bermuda Triangle . . . some irresistible force has everyone trapped.

He looks around at us all. There is menace in his laughter now. "This skill of mine," he asks us, "is it fake, or is it real?"

"It's—real!" Elegant scholars, grizzled elders, fair women and brave men, workers, students, housewives . . . probably butchers, barbers, retired officials, and peddlers as well . . . in this instant all answer in unison like children in a classroom.

"It's a real skill, so. . . . " He spits on the ground. "I asked for some money for an ice cream. Was I right to do that?"

"You—were—right!" We chorus obediently. Like someone waking from a dream, the thin man in the tortoiseshell glasses gropes all over his body. Finally he pulls a wad of tattered bills out of his pocket, selects a red one, and hands it over.

The Sichuanese smiles slightly. He holds up the red paper

and shakes it at the crowd. "See how generous our friend is! I ask for fifty cents, and he gives me a buck. But . . ."—there is a change in his manner as he continues, slowly and deliberately—". . . you earned this money with your sweat and blood. I know how it is for people in Shanghai. A university professor doesn't earn enough in a day for a pack of Marlboros—he certainly can't afford fancy neckties or a leather jacket. In the morning he only has rice gruel to eat. And you young ladies—you look so cute in your makeup and bright clothes, but all you eat for lunch is salted vegetable soup. So . . . how could I take this money? How could I?"

No answer. All these smart people are dumbfounded.

He snaps his fingers. The red banknote flies through the air, loops over, and lands at the feet of the thin man. Hesitant eyes peer through tortoiseshell frames, following the scrap of paper until it settles on the ground.

Hushed whispering begins. People are trying to work out whether they should stay or leave. The plump woman turns away, only to have him shout and point to her again. Her flabby body shakes with terror.

Nobody dares speak. All eyes are riveted on his other hand. He raises it slowly, his finger pointing at the young man in the Nikes. The pitiful youth stands like a statue, red pimples protruding all over his face, frozen in time.

What's he up to, this extraordinary stranger?

Finally his hand is drawn back. He taps another man on the shoulder: "Young fellow. . . ."

The man doesn't really look young, but then he isn't all that old either. He is dressed in an old blue police uniform and Chinese-made Liberation running shoes. He has a narrow forehead, a long chin, and narrow slits for eyes. He reacts quickly—before the Sichuanese can make his pitch, he has a five-yuan bill ready in his hand!

"Well, well! Another generous friend!" Again, he takes the banknote and gives it a shake. "He gives me five bucks when

I ask for fifty cents! I'd say that a man who's just out of jail is more free than anyone with his cash. . . ."

He murmurs to himself and squints at the man in the police uniform, sizing him up. "A man just out of jail is afraid of the cops. So he does what the hunters do when they want to fool a tiger. They drape tiger skins over themselves, and he puts on a police uniform. We know how it is! However . . ." —his voice becomes slower, the words drawn out—". . . how could I take your money? I can see your pocket bulging, but all that means is that you've made a bit of money and you don't know what to do with it. But that money wasn't so easy to come by. If you want to get a trader's license, you have to go to the Department of Commerce, the Tax Office, the bank, the Environmental Protection Agency, Public Security . . . one place after another, to get your forms stamped. You haven't made a cent yet, and the money's flowing like water. When you do finally make a little profit, you think you're in luck. But it's slippery, this luck! It can find you, but you can't find it! All of a sudden there's a new policy, and you find you didn't play your cards right. Screw up once, and you're back in the slammer. How can I take your money?"

Again the bill is tossed back.

Everyone is totally confused. It's like a play, him demanding money then giving it back. Everyone wants to act their part now, pulling out their money and offering it respectfully to him. And the amount they offer keeps increasing—perhaps because they're afraid of him, or perhaps because they hope he'll give it back. By the plump woman's turn, it's up to ten yuan. Frowning slightly, she brings out her money, staring anxiously at the outstretched black hand as if it were grasping her soul.

This time, to everyone's surprise, he doesn't return it. Instead, he stuffs her money into his pocket: "I won't insist on this dear lady taking her money back. But I won't spend it on myself! It will go to print more envelopes, so I can give more people medicine to cure what ails them. Then even more people will have good fortune! Aah!"

It is a long, drawn-out "Aah," like officials say when they are making speeches. The plump woman has disapproval written all over her face, but there's not much she can do about it. People glance uneasily at each other, wondering what other tricks he has up his sleeve.

"Let me tell you straight." He takes off his shabby straw hat, revealing the few sparse hairs on his little head. "I don't really need an ice-cream bar. You figure out how much you want to give me!

"I know what you're thinking now! 'Humph! This fellow's just here to cheat us out of our money after all!' You're so cheap, you Shanghainese! All you care about is making money off the other guy. Some tiny amount of money the size of a fly, and it weighs you down like a millstone! Getting you to do something for someone else is harder than climbing up to heaven! As long as you live you'll never believe that someone like me just wants to bring good fortune to others. I'll be honest with you—I'm not expecting miracles. But I will ask you this: What is it that makes you, as humans, different from animals? Does that ever occur to you? Don't you want something more from life than just food and clothing—like doing something for society, for humanity? There's a saying here in Shanghai: 'People need to know their own value.' Right? So, people, where do you find your value? Are you just working for yourselves and your children? I'm sorry to have to tell you this, but even if you're a Party member or an official, you're still no better than a beast! I'm not in the Communist Party myself, but I'm more of a Communist than most Party members. Why? Because I serve the people! That's how I know my value! To my mind, real human value is in doing good deeds for humanity, no matter how small. . . ."

His face is earnest now. Hat upturned in his hand, he steps toward us. There is a deathly hush. The greasy black hat is like an open mouth. Somewhere from the depths of that mouth comes a derisive, merciless laugh; the man's voice seems to drift in from far away.

"Today I will use my special powers and restore your power to you. Don't get me wrong! I'm not superstitious, and I'm not religious. I don't believe in any religion. I believe in humanity! Only in humanity! Now, if you please, grandfathers, uncles, tradesmen, and young friends, those of you who have received my medicine, a small contribution for humanity!"

First into the hat is a ten, and the man who puts it in is the released convict in the police uniform. His move acts like an order, as those who have received the envelopes push and shove each other to be first with their donations. In no time the hat is crammed with money, much of it in one-, two-, and five-yuan bills. There are very few small bills or coins. Nobody but the man in the police uniform has put in a ten, however—even in the general panic, the others have kept their heads somewhat.

"Master, can we go now?" someone asks timidly.

"Sure. Feel free to go." He becomes expansive. "Just as long as you understand how people ought to live their lives! Do as you please! I have other places to go to cure the sickness of humanity," he says, stressing that final word, *humanity.*

With these words, he clasps his shabby hat to his chest and heads for the road.

Three tall cylindrical trash cans stand at the roadside. The garbage in them has overflowed, and a small mountain of it is piled up on the curb. A woman dressed in rags squats by this pile of trash, picking through the rotting food and vegetable peelings with shaking hands. Whatever she finds, she drops into a worn bamboo basket.

The Sichuanese stands silently at her side. Then, without any warning, he leans forward and dumps the contents of his hat into her basket. Her scraps and peelings are covered with brightly colored paper bills.

The dispersing crowd forms again instantly. "What's his connection with the old woman? Do they know each other? Are they in this together?"

The old woman stares at him in disbelief and raises a hand toward him. Five blackened fingers stretch wide apart.

He looks down at her hand. A gentle smile lights his small eyes: "The money's for you." He puts his hat back on his head and walks away.

"Money . . . don't want. . . ," the old woman mutters. She shakes her head and pulls a banknote out of the basket, holds it up and strokes it, then lets it slip from her fingers onto the pile of trash. Still muttering, she picks the bills out one by one and throws them away.

"A madwoman." The people feel disappointed. They can't take their eyes off the banknotes, some stuck to bits of watermelon rind, some tucked under an old box, some teetering on top of the pile, about to flutter away . . . even in a pile of filth, money still fascinates them. Which one did you put in? Which one was mine?

They turn away from the money and look at the madwoman. Somewhere in their consciousness, a powerful force is holding them. Even if they know which of the banknotes is theirs, they don't feel it's quite right to be looking at it any more.

The old woman goes on hunting through the garbage, oblivious to everyone around her. Ignoring the money, she picks out the peelings and puts them in her basket, shaking off the dirt and the banknotes that are stuck to them.

Driven as much by pity as by curiosity, I too go over to look at the old woman as the Sichuanese had done. Looking at her untidy white hair, her sallow skin, and her thin lips, I feel the intensity of her hunger and thirst.

Slowly she straightens her back and holds up her hand. I pull out the bean-paste bun I was going to have for breakfast and press it into her hand.

"No! No! She jerks her hand away, then stretches it out again, five fingers outstretched. She waves them in my face: "Five languages! He speaks five languages!"

My bun has fallen onto the pile of garbage. I don't understand her.

"You can't execute him, comrade!" She seizes my sleeve. "Not now we have the reform policy. He speaks five languages; he can make a contribution to the country!"

She's grabbing me so tightly I feel uneasy and look around for help. They're laughing at her as they pull her away. Someone says, "Okay, we know now, five languages. Go home and get something to eat. Fat lot of use five languages are."

But the old woman doesn't want to go. She still resists and reaches out her arm to me, staring at me with dulled eyes. My heart is pounding—maybe what disturbs me is those eyes, sunken, opaque, glistening, like two coals glowing in a thick fog.

"Don't worry. She's harmless." A woman selling scallions and ginger by the road tries to comfort me. Seeing my bewilderment, she continues, "She must have done something terrible in a past life. Her son was executed ten years ago—he was a student at the Normal University. She's here every day, always says he never stole or looted, he was so honest and clever, but . . . it's politics, isn't it? Who knows what goes on?"

"Wang Shensheng!" I shout. "She must be Wang Shensheng's mother!" That's right! He was a university student, executed in 1977. I remember how everyone in the city was made to discuss the case. Full of righteous indignation, they all shouted, "Kill! Kill! Kill!" The muffled gunshot cast a dark shadow on the general euphoria that greeted the arrest of the Gang of Four. I had just started working as a junior editor at the Youth Press. When everything was quiet in the night, I would sit alone in the office, wiping away my tears as I wrote eulogies to the spirits of martyrs. At dawn, I would tear the pages into shreds and throw them into the toilet. My secret was discovered, but by someone who sympathized with me. He did not betray me, but jokingly recited a verse—I never knew where it came from—

Nobles strive for wealth and fame,
Heaven helps them all.
But still the anxious man from Qi
Fears the sky will fall!

Ten years have passed. The opinions that doomed Wang Shensheng to execution are now part of the state reform policy, proclaimed in endless propaganda campaigns. The people who were shouting for his death are now climbing the ladder of success, scrambling for official jobs and hustling for money . . . how absurd it all is!

I don't feel like giving up. I say to the people gathered round, "Her son was Wang Shensheng!"

People stare at me strangely, then walk off. To them, I am as mad as the old woman. I can't accept this. I grab hold of a fashionably dressed girl: "Wang Shensheng—did you hear?"

She giggles nervously: "Wang what? Is that some kind of disease?"

I hang my head, tell myself not to be so foolish. When I look up, the woman has gone, her bent body engulfed in the mass of humanity. My eyes cloud over, but still I can see a sinewy forearm and five fingers, pointing straight up to the blue of the sky like five stiff lances.

Author's Afterword

China is an agrarian nation, and peasants make up 70 percent of its billion or more inhabitants. The circumstances of the peasantry determine both the present social realities and the future of the nation. For this reason I resolved to direct my pen toward the villages. It is my intention to reveal both the strengths and the weaknesses of the national character through the life of the villages, to show historical changes in the fate of the peasants, to lay bare the suffocating brutality of traditional feudal culture, and to find the spiritual essence and cultural qualities of the Chinese people—and in so doing to search for the rules and directions for the future development of Chinese society.

I have set my stories in the eastern plain south of the Yangtze River, attempting to bring together the beauty and refinement of the natural environment and the historical destiny of its people. The language of my stories is based in the distinctive melodic speech of the peasants of this region.

I hope that through this volume of stories I might make a modest contribution to cultural exchange and mutual understanding between East and West.

Zhu Lin
Shanghai, April 1992

Translator's Postscript

Zhu Lin's Literary Mission

Almost two decades into her literary career, the talented and prolific writer Zhu Lin is virtually unknown in the West. Even in China, where she has published five novels and several volumes of short fiction and stories for children, she remains outside the circles of the most famous and favored. This qualified acceptance of so gifted an author results in part from Zhu Lin's personality: by nature melancholy and suspicious, she has neither the inclination nor the social skills to cultivate connections with those who might promote her writing. Furthermore, as the reader of these stories will observe, Zhu Lin takes a generally bleak view of Chinese society, especially its treatment of women, a position scarcely calculated to endear her to authority. Finally, she has made no attempt to conform to literary fashion, staying with a more realistic storytelling style while many of her contemporaries were experimenting with literary modernism learned from Western writers like Gabriel García Marquez.

Despite her relative isolation from the literary mainstream, Zhu Lin is one of the ablest of a remarkable generation of Chinese writers born as China came under Communist rule. They came of age in the turbulent years of the Cultural Revolution and were then banished from the cities to the poverty of the Chinese countryside before returning, in the cultural flourishing of the late seventies and eighties, to recount their own tribulations as well as those of the peasantry. Her novels and stories, many of them set in the Jiangnan region of east-central China where she now lives, chronicle the changes that the twentieth century has brought to a society still dominated by a stern and often cruel patriarchal tradition.

Zhu Lin was born Wang Zuling in 1949, the only child of parents who divorced in the first year of her life. She was raised by her father, a remote and eccentric academic, and his mother, in an atmosphere that she remembers as cold and loveless. As a member of the first generation educated under socialism, Zhu Lin read the literary works of Soviet and Chinese socialist realism as well as such Chinese classics as *The Dream of the Red Chamber* and fiction by nineteenth-century European writers like Balzac and Dostoyevsky. Such eclectic reading was no longer possible with the outbreak of the Cultural Revolution in 1966, when the products of both the past and the outside world were condemned. As a member of a family of intellectuals, with "overseas connections" (one uncle left China in 1948), Zhu Lin belonged to a group regarded with great suspicion in an age of revolutionary puritanism.

Her graduation from high school coincided with Communist Party chairman Mao Zedong's launch of the movement to send urban youths "up to the mountains and down to the villages," a policy designed both to rid the cities of lawless Red Guards and to reform the thinking of China's young people by immersing them in the practical values and austere work ethic of the peasants. Party propaganda boosted the rustication of urban youths as a glorious opportunity for reeducation and contributing to society; but for most of the more than twenty million urban youths who were "sent down" to the countryside, it was a time of deprivation, alienation, and suffering. Life in the countryside was particularly difficult for the women, many of whom were raped by those responsible for their welfare. Those who returned to the cities often found themselves victimized again, deprived of the chance for marriage and family life.

Zhu Lin was one of the first high school graduates from Shanghai sent to Fengyang, one of the poorest counties in Anhui Province, where she remained for six years. She has not written about her own rustication and is unwilling to speak of it, but the experience has greatly influenced her writing. Shocking as her portrayals of village life may be, Zhu Lin insists that she never exaggerated the hardships endured by either the urban youths or the peasants; on the contrary, she claimed in an early interview, had she described what she had witnessed in Fengyang in all its awfulness, her readers would not have believed her.

She returned to Shanghai in 1974 and was assigned work digging air-raid shelters. Fortunately for her, some children's stories that she had written were read by Zhao Yuanzhen, an editor at Shanghai's Youth Press. He managed to find her an editorial job there and has aided her subsequent career. While at the press, she completed her first novel, *The Path of Life,* working in secrecy for fear that she would be criticized by her colleagues, either for her ambition to be a writer or for her negative portrayal of the rustication of urban youths, which was still official policy at the time.

The Path of Life, published in 1979, was the first novel to reveal the dark side of the lives of young urbanites in the countryside. It set the tone for Zhu Lin's later writing in its somber view of society and its concentration on the plight of women; the difficulty she had getting the novel published, even in a bowdlerized version, was also a sign of awkward relations to come with cultural officialdom. Still, the novel launched her literary career: the next year she was sent to a training session for young writers (where her fellow students included Wang Anyi and Zhang Kangkang, both of whom are now also successful authors) and was subsequently transferred to the Shanghai Writers' Association to write full-time.

In 1980, Zhu Lin moved from Shanghai to Jiading, a county town in the semirural suburban sprawl to the northwest of Shanghai. It is a location that places the author where she belongs, poised between the country and the city, observing both but belonging to neither.

In her years in Jiading, she has written four more novels, numerous short stories and novellas, and several volumes of fiction for children. Much of her fiction, including the six stories included in this collection, is set in a literary territory that she has staked out for herself in and around the place where she now lives, a territory that runs from Shanghai (seen here in "Street Sketch") through the suburban counties ("Flap-Eared Hulk and His Bobtail Dog" and "The Festival of Graves") to the villages ("Snake's Pillow," "The Web," and "Night Songs"). This is Jiangnan, south of the Yangtze, a swath of land nourished by China's mightiest river as it sweeps through Jiangsu Province, past Shanghai, and out to the sea.

In the fiction of Zhu Lin, as in the popular imagination, Jiangnan is a Chinese Eden, a moist and misty plain interlaced with waterways lined with trees and bamboo (the author's pen name means "bamboo grove"). It is a fertile and abundant place, to which people flee in times of famine elsewhere, and from which banishment to the barren north is a fearful prospect. Zhu Lin shows us the people of the region as conservative and close to the land, living their lives to the seasonal cycle and depending on the bounty of nature and the goodwill of officialdom. It is a beautiful and serene environment, which provides an ironic backdrop to a human world that is often callous and cruel.

The principal division in Zhu Lin's Jiangnan is between those who have power and those over whom they exercise it. While the political changes of the moment affect the residents of the city and its suburbs, the villages remain in the enduring grip of tradition: the mighty retain their authority regardless of events in the outside world, and tragedies are destined to repeat themselves in future generations. Holders of power are typically male (Huang Huizhen in "The Festival of Graves" being a rare exception), greedy, and opportunistic, presiding mercilessly over a submissive peasantry. Their relationship with those below them, particularly when such people are young and female, is expressed in the metaphor of predator and prey, most strikingly in the image of the spider capturing smaller flies and sucking the life out of them in the final chapter of "The Web."

Throughout Zhu Lin's fiction we encounter young women whose chief characteristic is an innocence that makes them easy victims for men in authority. Beauty and innocence doom those who possess them, and the symbolic act in authority's treatment of these women is rape. Toughie, the central figure of "The Web," and two of the three women in "Night Songs" are raped, as are a number of young women in Zhu Lin's other stories and novels; in "Snake's Pillow" the protagonist Rice-Basket narrowly escapes the same fate but still finds herself the target of cruel gossip from those who condemn her for attracting her assailant.

"Snake's Pillow" ends with the myth that gives the story its title and the flower that is its central symbol. The myth of the snake and the flower provides an exegetical commentary on the tragedy that precedes it, but it also stands as an allegory for the pattern of relations between the sexes that holds good through most of Zhu Lin's writing. Male authority is represented by the phallic form of the snake, its potential for cruelty and deceit reinforced by the association of the devil with the serpent in the biblical story of Eden. By contrast, the flower demonstrates qualities that are explicitly female. The snake's pillow flower grows in the moist dark conditions that characterize the female principle of yin, and it is closely associated with female sexuality. The flower, we learn from the story, can heal the sickness of others, but she will not save herself—even when presented with the opportunity to be rid of her tormentor, the flower sacrifices herself to save the cruel snake from the hunter and is thereby doomed to an eternity of victimization.

As for the men in Zhu Lin's stories who are cast in the role, not of the snake, but of Adam, even those who wish to save women from their undeserved fate find themselves unable to do so: Big Fool in "Snake's Pillow" is scorned by reason of his retardation; Pots in "Night Songs" is helpless against a crowd of thugs. The forces that propel young women in Zhu Lin's fiction to disgrace and ostracism are stronger than anyone's attempt to thwart them.

An exception to this tragic pattern is "Flap-Eared Hulk," where misadventure and misrule are comic rather than tragic, where relations between the sexes are observed from a male perspective, and where the protagonist's vision of his destiny is perversely and unshakably optimistic. The story also differs in its presentation of a marriage that, while less than ideal, still has a measure of equality. "The Festival of Graves" also represents a departure, in that the arbitrariness of officialdom is seen, ironically, from an official's point of view: the retired Party secretary justifies forcing her stepdaughter into a third-trimester abortion on the grounds that it was Party policy: "Huang Huizhen was the kind of official who always has to take the lead in implementing Party policy and never invites the disapproval of her superiors." The author's detailing of Party excesses and her insights into the old-guard mentality demonstrate a continued testing of the limits of official tolerance. The sentence just quoted, and other passages deemed excessively critical, were excised by the editors of *Shanghai Literature,* the journal in which the story appeared; they have been restored in the present translation.

Zhu Lin has been much more adventurous in terms of content than style; although she experimented briefly with the stream-of-consciousness narration fashionable in the early eighties, she has generally stayed with a straightforward realism that emphasizes plot and character rather than seeking to intrigue or disconcert the sophisticated reader with more complicated surrealistic narratives, as do, for example, the modernists and postmodernists among her generation and the one that followed it. "Street Sketch," the latest story in this collection, represents a change of style, with its looser structure and intimations of supernatural power in its unorthodox central figure, the seller of quack medicines.

Zhu Lin is reluctant to theorize about her work, but a short piece she wrote in 1989 may provide some insight into her literary mission:

> Of all my memories, none affects me more than "summoning souls." I remember myself as a child, hair standing on end, skin in goose bumps, woken up in the middle of the night by drawn-out howls of anguish, accompanied by the screeching of owls. I asked my grandmother as she lay beside me: "What's happening?"
>
> "They're summoning souls," Granny said.
>
> "Why do they want to do that?"
>
> "Because after people's souls have left their bodies they get lost and can't find their way home."
>
> I was determined to find out what these "souls" were and how it was possible to summon lost ones back home.
>
> Finally my chance came. I was walking back from school at dusk one day when I heard in the distance those same drawn-out anguished calls. My heart began to beat faster, and I rushed in the direction of the sound. There was our neighbor Uncle Wang sitting astride the roof of his house, a broom in one hand and an old basket in the other. He was screaming, "Little Treasure! Come back!" repeating the words over and over again, and banging on the basket with the broom handle. At the same time there was a woman's voice answering him, apparently from the bamboo grove behind the house: "Coming back!"
>
> The sound was anguished, plaintive, fervent, mournful, more despairing than hopeful, their pleading stricken with

grief. It was like the howl of the wind, the call of a crane, a tiger's roar, a monkey's shriek. It spread far and wide, through the village and beyond. Everyone and everything seemed to have stopped to listen: no child cried, nothing stirred in the fields; without a sound the ducks and chickens made for their pens, the wild birds for their nests. Dogs and cats lying at home pricked up their ears. . . .

Ever since that time, I have believed that this is the most heartfelt, most passionate, and most mysterious sound that human beings can make. And I have begun to understand what it means to summon souls. . . .

In later life, through reading and personal experience, I came to realize that souls themselves are enigmatic and inconsistent. In historical and literary works, I observed people exhausting themselves, paying any price in the search for their own souls. For my part, having experienced political and economic changes—being sent to the countryside, the Cultural Revolution, reform, and liberalization—I searched my own mind and found that there were things that baffled me. For example, in the days when every political campaign involved the absolute repudiation of the one that preceded it, why was it that everyone caught up in the process, victimizers and victims alike, would all declare themselves in absolute agreement with every campaign? Why did they never seem to stop and reflect on all this campaigning and the effect it was having on them? . . . It suddenly came to me that our souls—mine included—had left our bodies and that we needed desperately to find them again!

So I began my search, using my pen to summon souls, and directing my attentions first of all to the souls of the younger generation, doing all I could to restore them to the bodies they had left. I think that with effort each of us, young or old, male or female, may yet become full and complete again.

And that, for me, is the significance of our lives, and it is the purpose for my writing.

This may well be as close as Zhu Lin will come to explaining her fiction. Her own measure of her success as a writer is not so much in the understanding she gives us of her world, or in our enjoyment of her craft, as it is in the extent to which she touches the souls of her readers and restores them to the bodies they have left.

A Note on the Translations

Snake's-pillow (She zhentou hua) first appeared in the magazine *Qingchun* 3 (1983); this translation was made from the volume of short fiction of which this story is the title work, *She zhentou hua.* (Jiangsu renmin chubanshe, 1984.)

The Web (Wang) appeared in *Xiaoshuo jikan* 4 (1980). My translation is from a version of that text annotated by the author, which restores two lines removed from the original. I have omitted a final paragraph added by the editors of the magazine. This translation first appeared (in slightly different form) in *Renditions* 16 (Autumn 1981), and is reprinted here with permission.

Flap-eared Hulk and his Bob-tailed Dog (Da erduo Ada he tuwei bagou) first appeared in *Baihua zhou* 1 (1981), and was translated from the mid-length story collection *Heaven and Hell* (Diyu yu tiantang; Henan renmin chubanshe, 1984).

The Festival of Graves (Guole Qingming hua bu hao) was published, after considerable editorial cutting, in *Shanghai wenxue* 12 (1987). This translation, which is from the author's original manuscript, first appeared (in slightly different form) in *Mānoa* 1 (Fall 1989) and is reprinted here with permission.

Night Songs (Yuzhou chang wan) first appeared in the Hong Kong magazine *Bafang* in 1988, and was translated from this text; the story was reprinted in the mid-length story collection *Tui* (Shedding Skin). (Shanghai wenyi chubanshe, 1989.)

Street Sketch (Jietou SKETCH) was translated from *Xiaoshuo jie* 3 (1989).